VESPERS RISING

RICK RIORDAN
PETER LERANGIS
GORDON KORMAN
JUDE WATSON

SCHOLASTIC INC.

NEW YORK TORONTO LONDON AUCKLAND
SYDNEY MEXICO CITY NEW DELHI HONG KONG

To all the young Cahills who helped with the hunt – RR

For the fans, past, present, and future – PL

For Rose Brock – GK

For David, Rachel, and Mallory,
the best editorial team in the world – JW

Scholastic Children's Books
An imprint of Scholastic Ltd
Euston House, 24 Eversholt Street
London, NW1 1DB, UK
Registered office: Westfield Road, Southam, Warwickshire, CV47 0RA
SCHOLASTIC and associated logos are trademarks
and/or registered trademarks of Scholastic Inc.

First published in the US by Scholastic Inc, 2011
This edition published in the UK by Scholastic Ltd, 2012

Text copyright © Scholastic Inc, 2011

Book design and illustration by SJI Associates, Inc.,
Keirsten Geise, and Cahrice Silverman

The rights of Rick Riordan, Peter Lerangis, Gordon Korman and Jude Watson
to be identified as the authors of this work has been asserted by them.

ISBN 978 1407 13570 0

A CIP catalogue record for this book is available
from the British Library.

Printed and bound by CPI Group (UK) Ltd, Croydon, CR0 4YY
Papers used by Scholastic Children's Books are made from wood
grown in sustainable forests.

9 10 8

www.scholastic.co.uk/zone

Damien Vesper didn't plan on killing anyone today.

It was a fine autumn morning. A crisp wind had blown away the fog, and sunshine sparkled on the Celtic Sea.

In the distance, the coast of the Irish mainland stretched out lush and green. All of that land, as far as Damien could see, had been controlled by the Vesper family for centuries. From this island, a mile offshore, Damien couldn't see his ancestral estate—a castle he hadn't visited in over a year. He couldn't see his peasants dying or hear them crying in their squalor and misery. He couldn't smell the stench of death. Far to the northeast, one pillar of smoke snaked into the blue sky—probably another village being burned—but otherwise everything looked peaceful and beautiful. No sign of the Black Death.

Damien sipped his mulled wine, enjoying the scent of clove and nutmeg. He found it ridiculous that in this modern age, the year 1507, he still had to flee the plague — the same sickness that had cursed Ireland in his great-great-great-grandfather's time. So many advances in the sciences since then, so many amazing discoveries, and still the plague hampered his plans.

But no matter. The Black Death couldn't touch him here. He simply left his lieutenants in charge on the mainland to collect his taxes. He ignored their nervous reports about the hundreds dying each week, his peasants' annoying pleas for help. He continued his work in peace, enjoying the acquisitions his agents sent him from across Europe.

He gazed at the woodblock-panel map now adorning his wall — a beautiful piece just arrived from France. Reports and sketches from Italy covered his desk. Damien searched the world for rare treasures and powerful secrets. Yet a single message whispered in his ear this morning by his neighbors' housekeeper might be more important than any intelligence he'd ever received.

Was it possible that the most powerful secret in the world, a bit of information that could help Damien realize his wildest ambitions, was hiding right under his nose?

This morning, he intended to find out.

His eyes drifted to the new mosaic on his ceiling: a circle five feet in diameter depicting the Vesper coat of arms, but it was more than decoration. He'd recently installed the trap for his amusement. He'd thought to try it out on some lazy servant or the next guard who fell asleep on duty. But now it would serve a much more important purpose. He would test his theory. If he was right, Damien Vesper might become the most powerful man in the world.

There was a rap at the door. His servant Balthazar stepped through, bowing low. "My lord, Gideon Cahill is here."

Damien smiled. He didn't plan on killing anyone today. But he did believe in being flexible.

"Show him in," Damien ordered.

• • •

Gideon was dressed in his usual peasant clothes—quite unbecoming for a man of his talents.

His hair was a swirl of wild gray tufts like a bank of storm clouds. His rugged face was darkened from years of brewing mixtures in a smoky laboratory. Chemicals had turned his frock into a palette of stains, and his forearms were covered with notes in Latin—reminders that Gideon would write on himself when he couldn't be bothered to find a piece of parchment.

Only Gideon's gold ring, a family heirloom much too fine for a peasant, marked him as a man of worth. And his eyes—still fierce and bright as ever under bushy gray brows.

Those eyes had first caught Damien's attention a decade ago, when Gideon Cahill stood up at the Christmas feast, at Damien's own table, and dared to correct him on a point of astronomy, citing some new work by a scientist named Copernicus.

Damien was not used to being corrected. He might have had Gideon flogged for his rudeness, but the intelligent gleam in Gideon's eyes gave him pause.

He remembered thinking: *Here is a man I could use. Not a sheep. A man of intellect.*

After the feast, the two of them had talked into the night, discussing learned subjects no one else in Vesper's miserable backwater domain could hope to understand. It had been the beginning of a rare friendship.

True, that friendship had frayed since the Cahills and Vesper and his household had fled to this island together. Sometimes weeks would go by as Gideon secluded himself in his lab, only sending notes to Vesper's manor when he needed supplies or money. If not for the Cahills' housekeeper, Maria, Damien would've been intolerably ignorant of Gideon's activities, but Maria was an imperfect spy at best.

The last time Damien had seen Gideon in person, about a week ago, Damien had been startled—even concerned—by how much his friend had aged. Poor, noble Gideon, who took the plague so personally and labored like Hercules to find a cure. He had looked no better than one of Vesper's serfs, broken from years of hard fieldwork.

But now . . . just as the housekeeper had reported, something about Gideon Cahill had changed drastically. Gideon stood straighter. His shoulders seemed broader. Was his hair actually darker? It seemed impossible, but Gideon Cahill seemed healthier, younger.

He's made something in that evil laboratory of his, m'lord, Maria had whispered nervously. *Sick for a while, he was. But now he's changed—turned stronger, quicker, even his hearing is uncanny! I heard him talking to himself about a formula, a concoction. He's taken to witchcraft, I fear. M'lord, it's not natural, the things I seen him do!*

Damien did not believe in witchcraft, but Maria's tone had been sufficiently alarming to get his attention. She'd spied on the Cahills' household for him for years but never once come to him in such a state of panic. Now, seeing Gideon in person, Damien's suspicions deepened.

"My dear Gideon." Damien clasped his friend's calloused hands. "Come, you must see my new acquisitions!"

Gideon scanned the room warily before stepping inside. Damien felt a twinge of annoyance. Another change in the past few months: Gideon seemed increasingly mistrustful, *actively avoiding Damien's company.* Damien couldn't abide the idea that Gideon might be hiding something.

He cloaked his anger with a broad smile and shepherded his friend into the study until Gideon stood just beneath the new mosaic crest on the ceiling.

"You see?" Damien leaned over his desk and spread out half a dozen charcoal sketches. "These are only quick studies, of course. But my agent in Florence tells me this artist, Leonardo, is a master and also quite an inventor of mechanical devices — which, as you know, are my passion. Leonardo just completed a portrait of Lisa del Giocondo. He calls it the *Mona Lisa*. I thought I might commission him to do a portrait of me, and while he's here, I can pick his mind for mechanical secrets. How does that sound?"

"Expensive," Gideon murmured.

Vesper chuckled. Gideon was never easy to impress, which just made Damien more determined to impress him — even if today might be the last time.

He pushed aside the Leonardo sketches. "Perhaps you're right. But surely you must admit *this* was worth the price."

Damien gestured grandly at his new wall map — a series of twelve woodblock panels showing the entire globe brightly painted in blue and green. "The newest, most accurate map *anywhere*, Gideon. It's an exact rep-lica of one just commissioned in the duchy of Lorraine. Fellow named Waldseemüller created it. What do you notice?"

Gideon's keen eyes studied the map for no more than a heartbeat. "The new continents. He has labeled them . . . America?"

"Yes, after that explorer Amerigo Vespucci. Seems a silly name to me, but no matter. Our world has officially expanded, Gideon! Don't you find that exciting? Think of all those lands to conquer, all those kingdoms of savages with riches beyond imagining. Spain is already becoming wealthy, you know, bringing back shiploads of gold and silver. I tell you, if a man had enough power, he could set himself up as an emperor in the New World. It could as easily be called Vesperia, eh?"

Gideon frowned. "It seems to me, Damien, that we have enough trouble caring for the lands we already have. Forty-three more of our villagers died this week, you know. We must find a cure for the Black Death, and I doubt the answer lies in this . . . *America*."

Again, Damien kept his annoyance in check. Gideon was the only one who would dare speak so boldly to him. In years past, Vesper had found his honesty refreshing. He even allowed Gideon to call him by his given name.

But now Damien wondered if he'd allowed Gideon too much familiarity.

Our villagers? These lands belonged to Vesper alone. And when had his friend become so narrow-minded? Vesper showed him the new continents full of thousands of would-be subjects—a world to be conquered—and Gideon was concerned about forty-three plague-ridden peasants.

"Well," Damien said breezily, "a cure would be admirable, of course, which is why I've provided you quite a substantial amount of funding. How goes your research?"

There it was again: that slight hesitation. Gideon was definitely hiding something. The look in his eyes was almost *fear.* And yet physically he seemed so full of energy, standing tall and straight. He fairly *radiated* health.

A formula, a concoction, the housekeeper had said. Interesting . . .

"It goes slowly," Gideon said at last. "The mercury is too poisonous. The iron solute does not balance the humors of the body as I'd hoped." He looked up, as if just noticing the mosaic crest above him. "More new artwork?"

Damien ignored the question, though he was conscious of the trap's release button built into the floor, just a few inches from his left boot. If things went wrong, Gideon was in the perfect position.

"Perhaps if you used live subjects," Damien suggested, "human volunteers, as I proposed—"

"No, Damien."

"We have more than enough to spare. And it would speed your work."

"Never."

Damien pursed his lips. After all these years, Gideon Cahill still mystified him. So dedicated to finding a cure, and yet he refused to do the logical thing and experiment on peasants. Unless, of course, he had already tested his cure some other way. . . .

"Then you have made no breakthrough?" Damien asked.

Gideon hesitated. "I have found no cure."

"Ah. But you've found something."

Gideon twisted his gold ring. "My lord?"

So now he addresses me correctly, Damien thought.

"I've known you for ten years, my friend," Damien said. "You are a man of many talents, but deception is not among them. You are a poor liar. You've found something important, using *my* fortune, using equipment and ingredients that *I* have provided from the far corners of the globe, using this refuge island in *my* territory."

"This island is Cahill family land, my lord," Gideon corrected, "granted to us centuries ago by the Gaelic kings. We invited you here, gave you the use of this manor house—"

"Yes, yes." Damien waved aside the technicalities. "But it is still in *my* barony, and you owe me allegiance. At the very least, you owe me the truth. What have you found?"

Gideon locked eyes with him, and Damien took an involuntary step back. Gideon looked terrified, but Damien realized Gideon wasn't scared of *him*. Gideon Cahill was scared of what he'd discovered.

"I would tell you, my lord," Gideon promised, "if I had discovered anything that would do you good. Believe me, I have not."

"I see." Damien felt his pulse slowing, as it always did when he had to use force. The anticipation of violence had a calming effect on him—like a form of prayer. "That's unfortunate, my friend. I don't claim your skill with alchemy. But I do conduct my own research with mechanics, as you know. Unlike you, I have no problem testing my inventions on live subjects. Let me demonstrate."

Damien stepped on the release switch, and the ceiling above Gideon collapsed.

It was one of Damien's simpler creations but still impressive. The attic above the Vesper seal held three limestone columns set a hand's breadth apart, each as thick and heavy as a ship's mast yet perfectly balanced, so that only the slightest linchpin was needed to keep them in position. At the flick of a switch, gears turned, an iron rod retracted, and the Vesper seal crumbled. The columns crashed down like the fist of God.

The sound was terrible. The columns shattered. Shards of rubble flew everywhere, shaking the entire manor. Underneath the collapse, Gideon should have been smashed flat.

Yet when the dust cleared, Damien saw Gideon Cahill standing five feet behind the wreckage, unharmed except for scraped and bleeding knuckles on his right hand.

My God, Damien thought. *It's true.* Despite himself, he laughed with delight.

He realized his mistake too late. Gideon moved almost faster than Damien's eyes could register. In a heartbeat, he had Damien pinned to the wall, his fingers around Damien's throat. Damien was not light, but Gideon manhandled him as if he were a straw-stuffed scarecrow.

"You try to kill me, my lord?" Gideon's eyes flared. "Then laugh about it?"

For a moment, Damien was too shocked to speak. Laying hands on a noble was punishable by death, and yet Gideon—the gentlest man Damien had ever met—seemed quite ready to break Damien's neck. Gideon's thumb and fingers pressed under his jaw. Damien's pulse throbbed. His vision began to darken. With a flick of his wrist, he managed to slide a knife from his sleeve, where he always kept it.

"Is it—worth the price—Gideon?" Damien gasped, barely able to speak with his windpipe constricted. He pressed the tip of his knife gently against Gideon's ribs. "Think carefully."

Gideon's grip tightened. His eyes were still full of murderous rage.

"We'll die together," Damien croaked. "But—won't end there. Your mother—in Milan. Your brother—in Dublin. Your wife and children . . ."

Damien watched Gideon's face as the meaning of his words sank in. It was risky, threatening an angry man, but Damien had to remind him whom he was dealing with. Damien's network of spies and assassins extended far beyond Ireland. He had many friends and many more well-paid lackeys who would not take kindly to their patron's death. Gideon knew that. If he killed Damien Vesper, the entire Cahill family would be wiped from the earth.

There was an urgent pounding on the door. Balthazar

burst in, sword drawn. "My lord, is everything—"

"Stay your hand!" Damien barked. He fixed his eyes on Gideon. "Everything is fine—isn't it, Gideon? A small disagreement. Nothing more."

Damien counted to five, wondering if each heartbeat would be his last. Finally, Gideon's angry expression turned to disgust. He released his grip and stepped away.

Damien sheathed his dagger.

He swallowed, struggling for composure. "You see, Balthazar? Now leave us."

Balthazar looked at his master in disbelief, then at the gaping hole in the ceiling and the shattered ton of limestone on the floor, no doubt wondering how this constituted a small disagreement.

"Y-yes, my lord," he stammered. He quickly retreated, closing the door after him.

Gideon kicked at the rubble, scattering mosaic tiles from the Vesper crest. "I once thought better of you, Damien. I thought we were friends."

"But we *are* friends." Damien spoke with more ease than he felt, knowing he must turn the situation quickly. "The columns were only a test that I knew you would pass. Tell me . . . how did you dodge them?"

Gideon balled his fists. "If you threaten my family again, if you lay a hand on them—"

"No, no, of course," Damien said hastily. "Spoken in a moment of anger! But back to the point—no man is so agile. Your bleeding knuckles . . . you actually *pushed* one of the stones aside?"

Gideon still looked ready to attack, but his civilized nature seemed to be reasserting itself, as Damien had hoped. Given a choice, Gideon Cahill would almost always choose talk over violence.

"I deflected a column," Gideon allowed, "*barely*. Or it would've crushed me."

Damien shook his head in wonder. "You instantly assessed how the stone was falling—its mass, its momentum, how best to apply force to change its course—"

"A simple calculation," Gideon grumbled. "You could do the math as well as I."

"But not so quickly," Damien said. "Not in a heartbeat. You demonstrated unnatural speed, strength, mental acuity. . . . What has changed you, Gideon? What concoction have you made?"

Gideon blanched. "How . . ." His expression hardened as the truth dawned on him. "Of course—Maria."

"Do not be too angry with her," Damien said. "She needed the silver. And her husband . . . well, he's been a guest in my dungeon for years. She really had no choice."

Gideon brushed the dust from his shoulders. "I should have known," he said bitterly. "Even with me, you use spies."

"Your mind is agile," Damien said. "You have apparently found a way to increase your perception. But even this cannot change your fundamental nature, my friend. You are too trusting. You see the best in people. It is your most glaring weakness. Now tell me, what secret have you uncovered?"

Gideon glowered at him. "I once believed you supported my work because you wanted a cure for the plague — because you wanted to help your people and build a better world."

"I *do* want a cure," Damien assured him. "It might safeguard my own life, for one thing. It would also be a valuable thing to sell. But what you've discovered is obviously of even greater importance. As for helping the peasants out of the goodness of my heart — please! If the Black Death has taught us anything, it is that life is cheap."

"It teaches us life is precious!"

"Bah. I am not interested in stopping death, only in . . . directing it. This cure of yours . . . well, it was potentially valuable, but now you seem to have stumbled on something quite amazing — something that could help me immensely. I am interested in weapons, my friend. Power! *That* is how I'll build a better world."

Slowly, Gideon's face turned waxy with horror. Damien had seen that look before on the faces of his test subjects as it slowly dawned on them that they would never be leaving his workshop. "You are truly evil."

"That goes too far, Gideon. Even for you. This alchemy you've discovered, the process for strengthening the mind and body — it could give me an army powerful enough to drive the English from Ireland at last. King Henry is old and weak. His lapdogs in Dublin have been powerless for years. With your formula and the weapon I'm working on, Gideon, I could invade England itself. And after that . . ." He swept his hand across his newly acquired map. "A whole world awaits."

Deadly silence.

Gideon wrapped his bleeding knuckles in the hem of his shirt. His hands were beginning to shake. Damien made a note of that, as he might with a test subject. Perhaps a side effect of Gideon's formula? He would have to find out.

"Damien, I'm going home now," Gideon said. "I think you should return to the mainland in the morning. You're no longer welcome on my family lands."

Damien felt a twinge of regret. So this was what it felt like to lose a friend. Such conversations they'd had in better times! Such excellent dinners! Peasants were easy to replace. Gideon Cahill would not be.

"You've known me for ten years, Gideon," he said. "Have I ever failed to get what I want?"

"Good-bye, Lord Vesper."

"Before I am done, you'll wish those stones had crushed you," Damien warned.

Gideon met his eyes one last time, but his expression held no more anger—only disappointment—as if he dared to believe this break was Damien's fault.

Gideon left without another word.

Damien cursed and overturned his desk. Secret reports and Leonardo da Vinci sketches fluttered through the air, slowly settling in the rubble of his limestone trap.

Damien had tried. Truly, he had tried to be reasonable. But sometimes even the best plans must change. Tonight, Balthazar might get to use his sword after all.

●●●

Gideon cursed himself for a fool.

He was well acquainted with Damien's ruthlessness, but he still couldn't believe his old friend had tried to kill him. Worse: Damien had tricked him into revealing his newfound skills. Gideon had had enough trouble keeping Damien in check the past ten years, quietly thwarting his efforts to gain power, using his influence to calm Damien's tempers and spare the peasants from the worst of his wrath. Now Gideon's new discovery had upset the balance. Far from being a gift, the serum could ruin everything.

Halfway across the beach, Gideon almost collapsed from a wave of nausea, worse than before. The side effects of the master serum were becoming more pronounced by the hour. He held up his hand, his knuckles still bleeding. A few minutes ago, he'd had the strength to crush stone. Now his fingers shook like an old man's. The more he used his new abilities, the more he deteriorated.

He needed twenty-four hours more to complete his new variation of the serum. Perhaps this time the balance of humors would be correct, and Gideon could counteract the damage he'd done to his body . . . if he *had* twenty-four hours.

Why couldn't Damien have waited another day before confronting him?

As the nausea passed, Gideon took a deep breath and tried to clear his thoughts. The morning was unseasonably pleasant. Waves washed against the rocks. Gideon could see the mainland clearly, but he knew that from the mainland, this island would not be visible.

He could not stand to think that this ancestral stronghold, a refuge for generations of Cahills, might soon be his grave.

A square mile wide, the island was shaped like a cupped hand, with a palm of meadows in front and a protective curve of sheer limestone cliffs along the back like a row of fingers.

Despite the island's size and the height of its cliffs, a rare combination of factors made it nearly impossible to see from a distance—a trick of the light, the way the stone and shadows mixed together, the reflective quality of the cliffs throwing back the color of the sea. Gideon's great-great-grandmother Madeleine, one of the last famous Celtic warrior noblewomen, had discovered this place quite by accident, and even though her descendants had studied science for generations since, none of them quite understood the optical illusion that caused the island to disappear.

Unfortunately, Gideon had shared the secret

location with his former friend, Lord Vesper. At the time, it had seemed like a worthwhile risk. . . .

He looked back at Damien's beachfront manor house—not nearly as fine as the Vesper family castle on the mainland but still a stately home of golden limestone and oaken beams. It had once been a simpler dwelling, the original Cahill home on the island, but Vesper had wasted no time remodeling. He'd added a boathouse, servants' quarters, a storehouse, and a smithy. Small boats waited at the dock for the baron's pleasure. Mysterious shipments arrived as the tides allowed, making Gideon uneasy.

He turned toward the back of the island—toward home. Nestled at the base of the island's cliffs stood the present Cahill manor, a simple but solid two-story oaken structure built by Gideon's grandfather. It had housed three generations of Cahills. At present it sheltered everything Gideon held dear—his wife, Olivia, his children, his alchemy lab, his research.

A simple footpath, less than a mile long, separated the Cahills from their neighbor Lord Vesper, but the path was overgrown with weeds. Every time Gideon walked the distance, it seemed farther. Each time, he found it harder to pretend friendship with the man he had once admired.

Gideon tugged at his gold ring—a memento from his only trip abroad, many years ago, to visit his dying father in Milan. Damien believed the ring was a family heirloom. In a way, it was. Gideon's father had given it to him on his deathbed. But Gideon doubted even his father, a true genius, had understood just how terrible the ring's secret was.

●●●

Twenty-four hours . . . Gideon's legs began to shake. He must try to finish the new variation of the serum. And he had larger priorities as well: protecting his family, protecting the secret formula. But convincing Olivia and the children would be almost as hard as outwitting Damien Vesper. He took a deep breath and headed for home.

●●●

The dining table was in the garden. For weeks, Olivia had been grumbling about the need to clean it. Apparently, she'd taken advantage of the sunny morning to do the job. She'd drafted the children to help. Gideon stopped at the edge of the apple orchard and watched, cherishing the sight of his family and dreading what he had to tell them.

Luke and Thomas must've just carried the massive table outside. Their clothes were soaked with sweat.

Luke — never one for manual labor — winced as he picked a splinter from his palm. He was the tallest and oldest of their children — twenty-three now, a man full grown, as he never tired of reminding them. Most young men his age would've been married with families of their own by now, but Luke was not one for domestic bliss. He griped constantly about the sacrifices he'd made, coming home from his studies at Oxford to help his parents, but truth be told, he hadn't done well at university. People outside the family tended to find him . . . unsettling.

He had Olivia's raven hair and Gideon's furrowed brow and preoccupied scowl. His frame was long and wiry, rather snakelike, and in fact when he annoyed his siblings (which was often) they called him "the last snake in Ireland." Gideon chided the younger siblings when they said such things, but as much as he loved his elder son, he couldn't help agreeing there was a disquieting quality to him. He tended to creep into places where he should not be, silent and cold-eyed, always watching, ready to strike if attacked.

His younger son, Thomas, was built more like a barrel maker or a barrel itself—stout, squat, and solid. Gideon had little doubt Thomas could've carried the dining table by himself, though it weighed several hundred pounds and was a good eight feet long. Thomas was only thirteen, but he'd beaten grown men at arm wrestling and once in a fit of rage had broken down a door with his head. His siblings joked that this had addled his wits, but Gideon did not agree. Thomas spoke rarely, and he might not be the quickest thinker, but he *did* think. Given time, he could work out almost any problem. At the moment, he was staring with distaste at a wad of oily rags his mother had given him.

"Go on, then," Olivia commanded. "Luke, you, too.

The table won't polish itself. And girls, for goodness' sake! Jane, come over here. Katherine, what are you doing?"

The girls were distracted as usual. Jane, the youngest at ten years old, was chasing a butterfly through the chrysanthemums. Quite late in the autumn for butterflies, Gideon thought, but leave it to Jane to find one.

She was a wisp of a girl with long straw-colored hair and eyes that seemed to drink in everything they saw. Her hands and dress were stained with paints. Gideon had to smile at that, as she shared his habit of writing notes and sketches everywhere, even on her arms and clothes.

Katherine, fifteen, was a different story. She'd plopped herself down cross-legged in the cabbage patch and was fiddling with the centerpiece from the dining table—a bronze astrological globe Gideon's father had sent them from Italy years ago. As always, Katherine wore a frock and breeches like a boy. Her dark hair was cut short. She was busily disassembling the globe, her fingers working at the joints and hinges. Perhaps Gideon should've been angry, seeing a family heirloom destroyed, but in truth he was surprised it had lasted this long. Katherine took apart everything, and Gideon understood. He'd been the same way at her age.

He stepped out from the shadows of the apple orchard, and Olivia noticed him first. As always, he caught his breath when their eyes met.

No matter that they'd been married twenty-five years. She was as beautiful and formidable as ever—her long curly hair still black as midnight, her green eyes still piercing. Gideon often reflected that the children had gotten their best qualities from Olivia. She saw value and beauty in even the smallest things, like Jane. She could fix nearly anything, like Katherine. If her family was threatened, she could be as dangerous as a coiled viper, like Luke. And like Thomas, she was strong willed and stubborn enough to break down any door—although she didn't need to use her head. One of her stern looks was usually quite sufficient.

She blew a strand of hair from her face and set her hands on her hips. "Well, Gideon Cahill. If you're done chatting with His Lordship, perhaps you'll help me with this unruly mob."

"Papa!" Jane beamed, holding up her cupped hands, in which she'd caught her butterfly. "Look what I found! May I paint its wings?"

"No, child." Gideon tried to repress a smile. "It would hurt the poor creature."

Jane pouted. "But I can make him much more colorful."

Katherine snorted, glancing up from her disassembled heirloom. "Don't be silly, Jane. You and your 'art' will destroy the world."

"Will not! And I'm not silly, am I, Luke?"

Gideon found it strange how much Jane adored her oldest brother, but then again, she could see the smallest good in even the most unlikely places. Despite his look of utter distaste for being here, in the bright sunlight, doing physical labor with his family — Luke managed a dismissive shake of the head. "No, Jane, dear. Your art, at least, never left something valuable in pieces."

Katherine's ears turned red. "I'll put it back together!"

"Like you did the miller's wheel last year?" Luke asked. "We had no flour for a month."

Thomas stepped toward him, pushing up his sleeves. He might've been ten years younger than Luke, but that had never stopped Thomas from a fight. "Leave her alone, Luke."

"Stop it!" Olivia ordered. "I won't have this at the dinner table!"

It was an absurd comment, as the dinner table was in the garden, but the children became quiet. They were used to their mother's cardinal rule: no fighting at the table. This was their neutral ground, their only place of peace.

"Now," Olivia continued, "we need to get this table cleaned. And no more fighting." She looked at Gideon for support.

"Your mother is right," he said. "But first . . . gather 'round, children. I have something important to tell you."

His tone must've been graver than he realized, because none of them argued. Jane let the butterfly go. Katherine set down the globe. The boys stepped away from each other warily. All of them approached the table, instinctively arranging themselves at their usual spots for dinner.

"Husband?" Olivia knit her brow. "What is it?"

"Children," Gideon said. "There may be some trouble ahead. You know of my alchemy work, my search to cure the Black Death."

"Does one of us have the plague?" Thomas asked with alarm.

Jane tilted her head quizzically. "No, I'd have noticed that. The complexion changes, the color of the eyes. Have you found the cure, Father?"

"No, it's something different," Luke guessed. "He's found something even more important."

Gideon stared at his elder son. "How do you know this?"

Luke shifted his feet. "Just speculation. I simply—"

"He was sneaking around last night," Katherine grumbled. "I saw him coming out of your laboratory, Father. He's *always* sneaking around."

"Liar!" Luke snarled.

Thomas grabbed for his brother, but Gideon shouted, "Stop! All of you!"

He tried to control the tremor in his voice. "Luke, you cannot enter my laboratory. It's wrong and it's dangerous. But that's not the most important issue at present. You've guessed correctly. I've found something— something I need your help with. All of you."

He reached under the edge of the dinner table and found the secret lever. The latch released, and four small drawers sprang open—one at each setting where his children normally sat.

"Father!" Katherine said with glee. She ignored the contents of the drawer, even though it glowed with a faint green light. Instead, she examined the drawer itself. "A pressure lock? A concealed trigger? This is brilliant!"

Jane gingerly picked up her own package—a parcel the size of a folded dress, wrapped in velvet, tied in twine. Tucked under the twine was a glass vial with a cork and a leather strap. Jane picked up the vial. Even in the bright sunlight, the liquid inside glowed, staining her fingers emerald green.

"It's beautiful," she murmured.

"Be careful, my dear," Gideon said. "That is your future."

"Husband!" Olivia warned. "This is too dangerous. You promised—"

"I promised only as a last resort, Olivia. Believe me, if there was any other way—"

"Father, what *is* this?" Luke demanded. He held up his own parcel, similar to Jane's.

Thomas held up his gift as well, a bulkier bag of

objects tied with a leather cord. His glass vial looked tiny and fragile in his massive hands.

"It's glowing," he announced.

Gideon ran his trembling hands along the scarred surface of their dinner table. He had a terrible suspicion this would be the last time they were here together. He saw the gouge Thomas's knife had made last Easter. He saw the red stain burned into the table from the time Luke had mixed herbs, wine, and rare chemicals stolen from the lab to make his own "plague cure" when he was ten. In another corner, Katherine had carved something that looked like a dragon. Gideon still remembered the conversation: *My dear, there are no such things as dragons.* She had looked up defiantly. *There should be. Perhaps I will build one some day.* Even young Jane had been quick to leave her mark. Her place at the table had been previously scarred from generations of Cahills, but she'd filled in those scars with various paints — as if color could heal — and created a web of beautiful lines.

Around this table, Olivia and Gideon had celebrated the birth of each of their children. To think that they might never be together again . . . He swallowed and braced himself for what he must do.

"Children, I need your help. We are in great danger. As you well know, I've worked many years attempting to find a cure for the plague. At first, I sought a way to kill the contagion. Then it occurred to me that perhaps the answer was instead to strengthen the body. If a man could be made more resilient, healthier, stronger in mind, body, and spirit, then perhaps the Black Death could not touch him. My approach had . . . unexpected consequences."

Katherine held up her vial with new interest. "A serum of some kind? To strengthen the receiver?"

Gideon glanced at Olivia. Her eyes were full of warning, but it was too late to turn back now.

"I discovered the formula quite by accident," he said. "In its combined form . . . it is very potent."

Jane's eyes widened. "You took it! You experimented on yourself. Last month when you were sick, it wasn't an illness, was it?"

Gideon shook his head. "I was terribly foolish, Jane. It almost killed me and—" He stopped himself before he could complete that thought: *and it still might.* "But when I rose from my bed, I found I had changed. I was stronger. More agile. My mind had a greater capacity for numbers. My memory increased a hundredfold."

"Excellent." Luke hefted the vial, a greedy light in his eyes. "And this is the serum? How can we be in danger, Father, if you are giving us such power?"

"I am *not* giving you such power," Gideon said. "What you are holding is not the completed serum. That is . . . not perfected yet."

As in fatal, Gideon thought bitterly, but he tried to keep his tone even.

"I am still working on the final variation of the formula," he said, "but for now the master serum is far too dangerous, especially if it were to fall into the wrong hands."

"Like Luke's," Thomas grumbled.

"Shut up, oaf!" Luke snapped.

"Children!" Gideon said. "Lord Vesper has guessed about the serum. He will stop at nothing to get it, and he cannot be allowed to have it. We have very little time."

Jane frowned. "But Lord Vesper is your friend."

"Foolish little sister," Katherine said. "His Lordship is no one's friend. He tolerates people as long as they are useful. And Father is very useful."

It was bitter to hear this from a girl of fifteen—bitter to think she had such a cynical view.

"Sadly, Katherine is right," he said. "Damien—Lord Vesper—has become too power hungry. He cannot be trusted or kept at bay any longer. Your mother and I feared this might happen, which is why I have divided my research. Each of you must guard the treasures I have given you—ingredients, tools, pieces of the formula. Your individual portions are not meant to make sense. I have intentionally obscured the means to re-create the complete formula. But taken together, reassembled properly with all thirty-nine ingredients, these treasures will yield the secret of the master serum. Until we can escape Lord Vesper's reach—"

"Wait," Thomas said. "What about these glowing vials?"

Gideon hesitated. His work was so complex few

adults could understand it, much less children. But looking around at his family, he knew he owed them complete honesty. More than that, he realized with fierce pride that all of them *could* understand. As different as they were, his children were all brilliant in their own ways. All of them were at *least* as bright as he was.

"Each vial holds an incomplete version of the serum," he explained. "Thinking of you children—how different you are and yet how gifted—is what inspired me to try the four-part approach. While the master serum is still imperfect, far too dangerous to take, the four strands separately are safe enough. Together, your four vials would re-create the master serum, but in an emergency, children—you might use your individual serums to give you strength, according to your natural talents."

"Give us the *master* serum," Luke said. "You took the risk and lived! Together, we would be unstoppable. We could overcome Lord Vesper easily."

Gideon shivered. His son's tone reminded him too much of Damien's. He could not tell Luke just how dearly his rash decision to try the serum had cost him. The new outbreak of the plague had given Gideon a sense of urgency, made him disregard caution and rush his research.

If I can save more lives, he had thought, *it will be worth the risk.*

Now he was paying the price.

"No, Luke," he insisted. "As I told you, the master

serum is much too dangerous. It is far too tempting for anyone."

"Except for you," Luke said.

"Luke!" Olivia chided. "Your father is trying to save our family as well as his work."

"But he doesn't trust us with his secrets," Luke said. "You've put us in danger. You want our help. You owe us the full power of your serum."

Gideon could see the other children tensing, watching this battle of wills. They had never seen Luke rebel so brazenly, but Gideon couldn't feel anger, only sorrow. Luke was suspicious, grasping, perhaps a little too much like Lord Vesper—but if so, it was because Gideon had not been there for him. He had been so absorbed in his work he hadn't been a proper father.

His children might be brilliant, but they were still children, even Luke. They were already scared. Gideon had to stay confident for them. He couldn't tell them about the unintended consequences of the master serum, about his own rapidly diminishing chances at survival. Unless he had twenty-four hours to complete the next variation . . .

"Of course," he agreed. "Children, I have complete faith in you. Working together, the four of you will do more than I ever could alone. You will perfect the serum and make sure it is used only for good. When the time is right, and you are far away from here, you can pool your resources and—"

"Where are we going?" Katherine interrupted. "And

why are you talking as if you aren't coming with us?"

Gideon forced a smile. "Of course I will come with you. But I want you all to get safely away first. Thomas, are the boats still in the cove?"

Thomas nodded, clearly mystified. Since the time of Madeleine, who'd discovered the island, all Cahills had been natural mariners. They learned to swim and navigate as soon as they could walk. The family kept three small boats on the far side of the island, ostensibly for fishing and amusement, but Gideon always felt better knowing they had a private escape route far from Lord Vesper's docks.

"Tonight," he said, "you will pack your things. Bring only essentials that you can easily carry—and of course the serums I have given you, well hidden in your bags. I will secure the laboratory to make sure none of my research falls into Vesper's hands."

"You mean you'll *destroy* the research?" Luke asked incredulously.

"Listen!" Gideon insisted. "We must not give any sign that we are fleeing. We will cook dinner as usual and spend the night so Lord Vesper does not grow suspicious."

"But why not leave now?" Jane asked.

Gideon glanced toward the house. In the window of the upper bedroom, the housekeeper Maria's face hovered like a pale ghost, watching. She would not leave until nightfall, when she would return to her own cottage near Lord Vesper's house. Five years she'd been with the Cahills . . . five years on Damien's payroll of spies.

"We cannot give Lord Vesper any reason to suspect we are fleeing," he repeated. "His guards on the island are more than capable of stopping us. And on the mainland . . . his reach is long indeed. We must get as far away as possible before he discovers our plan."

"Just before dawn, then," Thomas said. "That's the next time the tides will allow us to leave safely, at any rate."

Gideon nodded, grateful for Thomas's practicality.

He didn't add the last reason he needed more time. He had to continue his last attempt to perfect the serum. He might not succeed, but he had to try. And that meant he would have to stay longer than his family.

"In the morning, then," he said, "just before first light, you will make your way to the boats and head to the mainland. I will stay behind and buy you as much time as I can. At my first opportunity, I will make some excuse to visit the mainland, then meet you on the road to Cork. By the time Vesper discovers we're gone, we'll be far beyond his reach."

"But what if it doesn't work?" Jane's voice quavered. "What if Lord Vesper won't let you go? What if Lord Vesper stops us and searches us?"

"It will work, my dear." Gideon tried to sound reassuring. "I'm giving you the elements of the formula for a reason. Even if he found you, Vesper would probably never think to search you. He has no children and does not approve of children. I don't think it would ever occur to him that you might hold something of value."

No one argued this point. In all the years Vesper had been their family "friend," he never seemed to remember the children's names. To him, they were like cats—of some limited value, to be tolerated but not worth noticing, much less naming.

Olivia rested her hand on his arm. "Yes, husband. We'll do as you say. Won't we, children?"

They all nodded, though none of them looked comfortable with this plan, even Olivia.

"I can say no more for now," Gideon insisted. "Go to your rooms. Be prepared to leave, but for God's sake, children, be careful. Do not pack until Maria leaves for the evening. Do not say or do anything to make her suspicious."

"But why?" Jane asked.

He cleared his throat. "Maria . . . Maria would worry if she knew. Now go. And guard these packages with your lives."

To his relief, the children obeyed. Nervously, they clutched their newfound treasures and headed for the house in a group—looking for once like they had a united purpose.

Olivia turned toward him once they were alone. "Gideon, I don't like this plan."

"We agreed—"

"And I will support you, but there *must* be another

way." She rubbed her stomach as if it had begun to hurt. "There are . . . there are factors we haven't discussed."

Something in her voice troubled him. "What do you mean?"

"I just . . ." Whatever she was going to say, she apparently changed her mind. "We can't simply leave this island for Vesper to take. It's our home. It's been your *family's* home for generations. And the ring. I know you said never to speak of it, but—"

"I will send it with you to the mainland," Gideon promised, though the idea chilled his blood. Olivia was the only person he'd told about the ring's terrible secret, but asking her to carry that burden seemed unconscionably risky.

"You have to take the children away," he said. "Vesper will never stop. Even with my new strength, I can't fight an entire barony. Our best hope is to get far away from him and convince him that my research went up in flames so it's beyond his reach forever."

"But the research is in your *head,* Gideon. How will you get away—"

Gideon leaned forward and kissed his wife. She smelled of wholesome things: sunlight and clean wool, fresh baked bread and rose petals. He had not told her just how sick he was. It was all he could do to stay on his feet, to control the trembling in his limbs. Even if he finished the serum, he doubted it would be in time. His heart was near breaking, but he managed a smile. "Trust me, sweetheart. We will all be together again."

Before he could lose his nerve, he turned and walked toward the house, where his laboratory waited.

• • •

It was near midnight when Gideon realized he would not live to see the dawn.

He'd spent the entire day collecting his equipment, accounting for every scrap of research. He'd kept out only the essential beakers and distillation equipment for the final iteration of the serum. Every so often he'd turn and watch the drops of fluid traveling through the glass tubes with painful slowness. He wished he could speed the process, but there was simply no way.

In the meantime, he had prepared his last line of defense. He'd mixed niter, coal, and sulfur, pitch and acid — using all his alchemical training and his new-found quickness to create one final, deadly compound. Now sealed vats of explosive were placed around the laboratory, strung together with fuse wire of gunpowder-coated rope. On the table, his oil lamp burned with a low blue flame. A windup timepiece turned gears that held the end of the fuse, bringing it ever closer to the fire.

In the morning, Gideon would visit Damien's manor again. Hopefully, the serum would be done by then, and Gideon would be healthier, ready to take on his old friend. He would try to keep Damien engaged in negotiations for at least an hour — enough time for his family to get a head start on the mainland. Eventually,

Damien would grow impatient and demand to see Gideon's lab. Gideon would stall as long as possible, then reluctantly agree. If his timing proved correct, they would be almost to the laboratory when the time-delayed fuse ignited. Twenty explosive vats would erupt simultaneously, turning the house into an inferno, reducing this lab to a mound of ashes. There would be nothing left for Damien to find.

Perhaps Gideon could escape somehow later on, bide his time pretending to work for Vesper. He could find a way to reunite with his family eventually. Or if not . . . he would do whatever he must to keep Damien from getting the serum.

And the ring. Gideon cursed himself. He'd forgotten to give Olivia the ring, which was almost as important, almost as dangerous as the master serum.

He'd explained its secret to Olivia long ago and warned her that Damien Vesper should never possess it. She'd argued many times that the ring shouldn't be kept under Lord Vesper's nose, but Gideon felt he had no choice. He couldn't let something so dangerous out of his sight. Gideon had told Olivia to downplay the ring's significance should Damien ever ask about it.

Tell him it has sentimental value, he'd suggested. *Perhaps an heirloom from your family, which you gave to me as a token of our marriage.*

Now he would have to give her the ring and hope she could take it to safety.

Gideon looked around one more time, taking stock

of the place where he'd worked so many years. The laboratory took up half of the house's ground floor, but it might as well have been a separate building. A small side door led into the house proper, though Gideon usually came and went through the back exit, which led straight to the meadow. While Olivia and Maria kept the rest of the house well scrubbed and tidy, they were not allowed in the lab. For safety, Gideon forbade anyone but himself to enter. He kept the doors locked, thank goodness. If Maria had had a key for the lab, she might've given Lord Vesper *much* more information.

The lab's oak-beamed ceiling was low and blackened from years of smoke. Shelves of chemicals and racks of tools covered every bit of wall space. The waist-high worktables were cluttered with bowls and vials, and the room had no chairs. Gideon never sat while he worked. His spirit was too restless. He would pace between projects, checking on several boiling vats at once. Olivia often teased him that he cooked six times more than she did and still couldn't make a decent stew.

He was about to reset the timepiece, douse the oil burner, and close up the lab when a voice spoke behind him: "Father."

Luke had slipped through the interior doorway, which should have been impossible. Somehow, he'd managed to undo Gideon's foolproof bolt system. Now he stood there fully dressed, looking agitated.

"Luke?" Gideon managed. "What are you—"

"They're coming, Father!"

"What do you mean? Why aren't you in bed?"

Luke waved the question aside. "Couldn't sleep, of course. They're *coming*! Vesper and his men. You have to . . ." Luke glanced around the laboratory. He noticed the sealed containers, the fuses, the timepiece and burner, and with unnerving quickness he seemed to understand his father's plan.

"A time-delay explosion," Luke said in amazement. "You'll destroy the house, the formula—everything. But there's no time for that, now! The enemy is almost—"

A fist pounded on the lab's exterior door. Gideon's heart crawled into his throat. His enhanced senses should've registered the danger much earlier, but the same serum that had made him formidable was now betraying him, making his mind go fuzzy. Of course he should've realized: Lord Vesper had scented his prey. He wouldn't wait until morning. He would strike while Gideon was still unprepared.

"Luke, get out of here," Gideon ordered. "Wake the others and sneak away *now*."

"Give me the full serum!" Luke pleaded. "I can help you fight!"

He's already taken his fourth of the serum, Gideon realized. That explained how he sneaked past the security measures so easily. It explained the swift new cleverness in his eyes—how he had picked out details in a dark room and immediately reconstructed his father's plan. Luke had always been impetuous, but taking the serum? An unforgivable risk.

Still, at the moment Gideon was glad for his son's recklessness. It might allow him to save the rest of the family.

The exterior door shook again under the pounding of metal-clad fists.

"Luke, listen to me." Gideon grasped his shoulders. "Even together, we cannot defeat Vesper and all his men. He has assassins everywhere. I *know* what I'm talking about. Your only hope is to leave now. Wake the family and get out!"

"But the others won't trust me!" Luke said. "They never do. And how will you get away?"

Gideon didn't answer.

Luke's face paled. Gideon could see comprehension dawning on him. "Father, the master serum . . . you said it was too dangerous. You meant *fatal,* didn't you? You're dying . . . ?"

"You must protect the family now."

"But—"

"Go, Luke."

The door rattled and the hinges creaked.

"I love you, Father," Luke said, his voice wavering. Then he slipped inside.

Gideon barred the door and reset the bolts. He could hear Luke moving heavy furniture to blockade the other side.

Then the exterior door shattered, and two of Vesper's guards stepped into the laboratory.

They were both dressed in steel and leather brigandine armor. Vesper's lieutenant, Balthazar, stood at the right, his sword unsheathed. On the left stood the baron's executioner and strong-arm enforcer, who went by the name of Craven, though it did not fit his appearance. His eyes were a frightening milky white, and his arms were as thick as fence posts. His battle-ax was flecked with splinters from breaking down the door.

Lord Vesper himself stepped through next, dressed in black robes and chain mail. Damien was older than Gideon by at least five years, but he had no hint of gray hair, nor a wrinkle. The commoners swore Lord Vesper had made a deal with the devil to stay young. If Gideon had been superstitious, he might have agreed. The lord's curly black mane, handsome face, and dark, hungry eyes had not changed in a decade.

"Good evening, Gideon." Damien tugged off his gloves and scanned the lab. His eyes fixed on the nearest worktable, where Gideon's distillation was in progress and his texts neatly stacked. "Thank you for compiling your research for us. It makes things much easier. And that would be the mysterious concoction? Excellent. Balthazar, if you please . . ."

Before the lieutenant could step forward, Gideon grabbed the end of the fuse wire. He held it within an inch of the burner's flame.

"Come any closer," he warned, "and you all die."

Balthazar snorted and started to advance.

"Wait," Lord Vesper commanded.

Damien's keen eyes examined the scene more

closely—the incendiary charges, the wires connecting them, the timepiece and burner. Only Gideon's own daughter Katherine could've rivaled Damien for mechanical genius. The baron's lips curled into a dry smile as he appreciated the trap Gideon had created.

Balthazar waited uneasily, no doubt wondering why he was being held at bay by a crazy old alchemist with a piece of rope.

Damien tutted with disappointment. "Really, Gideon, are you willing to destroy yourself, your family, and your precious research? Would you sacrifice everything you've worked for just to thwart me? There is no need for that."

"I can't let you have the formula, Damien. It will die with me."

Damien tried to read his face. Gideon had seen him do this with so many people over the years. No one in his right mind would gamble with Lord Vesper and certainly not try to bluff him. Gideon was not bluffing, but Vesper would have trouble believing that. Self-sacrifice was a foreign concept to the baron.

"Work with me," Vesper said. "We can both benefit. When I am the most powerful man in the world, you will have every resource at your disposal for your projects. You can eradicate the Black Death, as you've always dreamed."

"And see the world crushed under your boots? No thank you."

"Your family . . . I can keep them safe, Gideon. But if you oppose me—"

"Do not threaten them again," Gideon growled. "They know nothing of my work, and I'll never let you use them as hostages to force my cooperation. I would rather die."

"I do not believe you," Vesper said coldly. "We will take your research. Step aside, and we will spare you."

He's lying, Gideon realized. Damien had come to the same conclusion as he: They were now archenemies. One of them must die. If the lab was intact, Damien was more than capable of understanding the serum notes. He had no need of Gideon. He would simply take what he wanted.

Whatever happened, Gideon was doomed. Even if he survived this night, he would never have time to perfect the master serum. The flawed mixture in his veins was already destroying him. The only thing left was to make his death count—to buy his family a chance at survival and to thwart Damien Vesper's plans.

He prayed that Luke had gotten the family safely out of the house. If they could make it to the boats, they had a chance. Someday, they might be able to reconstruct his research and finish the master serum.

So many things undone, so many possibilities crushed. Gideon would not see his children again in this life, nor would he be able to give the ring to Olivia. He could only hope that the ring would be buried with him, and his family would live.

"I have wasted enough time with you," Vesper snarled. "I will wait outside. Balthazar, Craven, I will count to sixty. At the end of that time, I expect Gideon Cahill lying at my feet—dead or alive, I don't care which. And do not let him damage *anything* in this laboratory."

Vesper swept out of the room.

Balthazar and Craven both stepped forward.

"Do not," Gideon warned them. "Vesper left because he knows you may die. Leave now. I have no wish to kill you."

Craven made grunting sounds like a pig—possibly his way of laughing. Balthazar sneered and raised his sword.

I'm sorry, Olivia, Gideon thought. *God protect my family.*

Gideon thrust the fuse into the burner. Lines of fire raced through the dark laboratory, and the world exploded around him.

• • •

Luke almost believed they would make it.

He'd managed to rouse his mother and siblings from their sleep and herd them from the house, telling them that Father had ordered them not to wait for him. Luke's tone was so insistent, so earnest, that not even his mother hesitated.

They'd followed Luke toward the cove, stumbling along in the dark, clutching their parcels of secrets and whatever other bags they could easily carry.

Halfway to the boats, they heard the explosion.

They all turned, their faces suddenly awash in red light from the distant fireball. Mother let out a sob of horror.

"Keep going!" Luke shouted. His heart was as heavy as iron. He knew exactly what had happened, but he could not let his father's sacrifice be in vain. He *had* to save his family.

"Father!" Katherine screamed.

She dropped her bags and ran for the house, but Luke grabbed her arms. "Stop it!" he cried. "You can't help him!"

Mother was already running. Thomas—the stupid oaf—shoved Luke aside, and he and Katherine raced after her.

Only Jane stood still, staring at the distant flames as if trying to understand who had painted them. "Luke . . . wh-where is Papa?"

At that moment, Luke felt ten years old himself. He wanted to weep. He wanted to scream in rage and frustration. But he had no choice. He had to be the adult now.

"It will be all right." He took Jane's hand. "I'll protect you. But first, come. We must help the others." Together, they followed their family back toward the house.

The fire was too intense for them to get close. White-hot flames danced across the timbers and ate through the walls like cocoon silk. Thomas tried to charge in, but Katherine and Olivia pulled him back.

"We must get help!" Katherine screamed. "Thomas, run to Lord Vesper."

"No!" Luke said. "Vesper was *here,* Katherine. This is his doing!"

Mother fell to her knees and wept. Jane hid under the dining table, which still sat in the garden. She hugged one of the table legs as if it were the mast of an unsteady ship.

Thomas stormed toward Luke. His face was blackened with soot, and his tears made red lines down his cheeks like ancient Celtic war paint. He may have been only thirteen, but the look in his eyes made Luke take a step back. Luke hated himself for feeling afraid, but his younger brother had always intimidated him.

"You're lying!" Thomas yelled. "You got us out of the house. You knew this would happen!"

"No, I—I suspected," Luke said, "but Father's orders—"

Thomas pushed him to the ground. "We could've helped him! You led us away and let Father die! Perhaps *you* started the fire!"

Luke felt as if the flames were inside him now, eating through his skin, consuming him with anger. The ringing in his ears, which had started as soon as he took his portion of the serum, became louder.

"I saved your lives, you fool!" he snarled. "Father was dying anyway! Don't you see that? The master serum made him sick. He was trying to keep Lord Vesper from taking our secrets. He died to give you time to escape. And now you stand here arguing with me when you should be running! You aren't even smart enough to save!"

Thomas charged, but this time Luke was ready. His little brother seemed to move in slow motion. Luke could not match his strength, but he used Thomas's momentum against him. He raised his feet, planted them on Thomas's chest, and rolled backward, sending Thomas flying over him and crashing into the dining table.

"Stop it!" Mother screamed.

Jane started crying. Katherine covered her ears and stared at her brothers in shock.

Thomas was crumpled against the table. Luke stalked over, turned him on his back, and placed his elbow against his brother's throat.

"I am *done* with you!" Luke bellowed.

All his rage boiled to the surface: the teasing he'd endured from the villagers for years, the jeering from his fellow students at Oxford, the suspicious looks from his own family. No one ever trusted him. He'd always been the odd man out, the strange, quiet child with the shifty eyes. Now he'd tried to do the right thing. He'd obeyed his father, spoken from his heart, and tried to save his miserable family. And they blamed him for the disaster!

Thomas's eyes bulged. He choked, grasping weakly for Luke's face, but Luke was too slippery for him to grab.

That's right, Luke thought. *You call me a snake? I'll prove I'm just as dangerous!*

"Stop it!" Jane shrieked. Luke realized she was pummeling him with her tiny fists. "Stop it, Luke!"

Stunned, he released Thomas and stepped away. Katherine rushed to his aid. Their mother simply stared in horror.

For a long while, no one spoke. There was no sound except the roar of the fire. Luke stared at his hands, suddenly overcome with shame and self-loathing. He had almost killed his brother. Was this because of the serum, or had this evil been inside him all along?

He looked at his family's terrified expressions, and he realized something more important than the house had been destroyed tonight. Their trust, their love—whatever mutual bond had held them together around this dinner table for so many years—had died along with their father.

The flowers blackened, the vegetable garden smoldered, and their family home collapsed in a roar of white heat.

"It was Vesper," Luke said stubbornly, though he knew it wouldn't matter.

Thomas rubbed his throat. His eyes still looked too large for their sockets. He said nothing, but Luke read his expression perfectly: *Your fault. All your fault.*

This time, Luke controlled himself. The serum was working its way through his body, slowly enhancing his senses, his understanding. He could see five or six moves ahead, as if the world had become a chess game. He knew anger wouldn't serve him now. He might as well argue with the flames as argue with Thomas. He needed to withdraw, find a safe haven, study his father's research. He could not stay here. And he certainly couldn't trust Thomas or Katherine.

"I tried to save you all," he said. "I tried to obey Father's orders. None of you would listen. So I'm going."

"Going?" Jane looked on the verge of tears again. Luke's resolve weakened. He couldn't stand to see his sister in pain, but he also couldn't travel the world with a ten-year-old girl in tow.

"Perhaps we'll see each other again, Jane," he said half-heartedly. "Mother will look after you. . . ."

His voice trailed off. One look at Mother's face told him she was in no condition to tend to anyone, even herself. Luke had seen that look too often on plague survivors throughout Ireland and England. He had seen the hollow-eyed women who had lost their entire families, their entire villages. Olivia Cahill might as well be a ghost herself.

He met Thomas's and Katherine's eyes one last time, and they silently agreed on one thing: their mutual hatred.

"Good-bye, then," Luke said. He turned and walked into the darkness.

He heard Jane crying, calling his name. He waited for the others to call him back, to realize their mistake and beg him to stay. But they never did.

• • •

Olivia grieved alone.

In the morning light, the ruins of the house looked like a black and shattered eggshell. Smoke still burned in her lungs, but her eyes were so painfully dry she could not cry.

She had wrapped Gideon in a singed linen sheet, his head cradled in her lap. She stroked his hair, willing him to open his eyes, but of course he did not. By the time she had found him, he had breathed his last. The flames had not killed him, but the heat and smoke had. Two other men had died in the fire. They had been badly burned, but Olivia recognized them as Vesper's guards—Balthazar and Craven. This had given her a steely anger to counter her grief and enough strength to move their bodies. Ironically, they had fallen across Gideon—perhaps trying to tackle him to prevent him from escaping. They had shielded Gideon's body from the worst of the flames. He looked remarkably peaceful. His hair was so sooty and scorched that he appeared young again—all the gray burned away.

Her fingers trembled as she caressed his brow. She wanted to shout at the sky. She wanted to curse Gideon for leaving her. But she couldn't blame him, even now. She had known when she married him: His heart was too big to be constrained. He cared for her deeply, but he cared for all humanity, too. He could never give up his mission to improve the lot of the poor and sick, to defeat the plague once and for all. He would do anything to save others. He had died—the stubborn, infuriating, gentle man—because he believed it was the only way to save his work and his family.

"Gideon," she said, trying to keep her voice from breaking. "The children are gone. I couldn't stop them."

Surely Gideon hadn't meant for that to happen.

Shortly after Luke had left, Jane had chased after him. Neither had returned. Olivia had finally shaken herself out of her misery and sent Katherine to find them. A half hour later, Katherine had returned and reported that a boat was missing from the cove. Luke and Jane had apparently made good their threat and left for the mainland.

Thomas and Katherine's grief quickly turned to anger. They blamed their father for not telling them everything, for trusting Vesper and Luke. They blamed Olivia for not stopping Gideon's madness. Luke and Jane had the right idea, they decided. It was time to leave this cursed family.

Their harsh words stung Olivia. She pleaded with them to stay, but Thomas and Katherine were soon gone as well. Olivia's spirit was so shattered she did not even follow. She stumbled toward the ruins of the house, hoping against hope that she would find Gideon alive. She needed his strength.

Now Olivia was absolutely alone. Or almost so. She hugged her barely swollen belly—praying the unborn child was still safe.

Gideon and the children hadn't known. She'd been waiting for the right moment, sensing that the stress in the family was too great to break such news. But if she'd told Gideon sooner, would he have been more careful? Would he still be alive?

A fresh wave of guilt washed over her. A fifth child on the way, and now she was a widow. Her other children had fled. She prayed they would come back when their grief and anger subsided. Surely they would not leave her for good.

But something told her that their family had permanently shattered. More important—the future of the entire world had splintered. Together, her children might've completed their father's work. Separately, they had gone into the world with secrets powerful enough to change history. Judging from what Gideon had told her, each of them carried a serum that would fundamentally alter their chemistry, instilling greatness and talents to them and their descendants for generations to come. They might be saints or monsters, kings or villains, but Olivia feared that separately, the children of the Cahills would never achieve Gideon's dreams. They would keep fighting, struggling with one another as they had always done, but now their squabbles would shape the course of civilization. The world would be their battleground.

We will be together again, Gideon had said—a cruel last memory of her husband. She looked down at his lifeless form and clasped his fingers. His gold ring glinted, its strange rows of engraved symbols even more pronounced with soot filling the grooves.

RICK RIORDAN

Many times she'd pleaded with Gideon to hide the ring or send it away, but he'd insisted that he could only keep it safe by keeping it close. Now that burden fell to Olivia.

Above all, Lord Vesper must never have it, Gideon once told her. *If he asks about it, tell him it has sentimental value. Perhaps an heirloom from your family, which you gave to me as a token of our marriage, eh? Perhaps that will keep him from demanding it. The man is like a crow. Shiny things catch his eye.*

Olivia's eyes fixed on the golden band. Blood rushed in her ears, and she was so overwhelmed with dread and grief that she didn't hear the approaching footsteps until Damien Vesper said, "My dear Olivia. I'm so sorry."

●●●

Vesper so rarely spoke to her, at first she was too aston-ished to respond.

He was dressed in black velvet, with soft leather boots and a silver chain around his neck. His expression was appropriately mournful, but his eyes were bright and greedy. *Like a crow,* Gideon had remarked.

Vesper's hand rested on the pommel of his sword. She noticed his eyebrows had been scorched clean off. Behind him stood two guards—men she'd never seen before. Already he'd replaced the two he'd lost in the fire.

"You demon," Olivia spat. *"You* did this. Your men are in the ruins, dead. You killed my husband."

Vesper's expression hardened. "I assure you, madam, I did not. As for my men, I'm sure they came here to help. I grieve as much as you do. I consider this fire a great tragedy."

Olivia realized that he meant it but for all the wrong reasons. He cared nothing for his dead servants. He barely looked at poor Gideon's body. Instead, Vesper was mourning the ruins of the lab—all those valuable secrets gone.

"Gideon thwarted you," she said. "Whatever you were looking for, it's been destroyed. Though I suppose you'll want to pick through the ruins yourself."

He met her eyes. Olivia did not flinch. Vesper had a reputation for reading faces, but Olivia was an actress of great talent. She'd grown up in a family of older brothers, all of them smart and strong. She could lie as needed, and swaggering men like Lord Vesper did not scare her.

"You know of Gideon's research, madam?" he asked.

"I'm a woman," she said flatly. "What would I know of such things?"

Vesper hesitated, then nodded. Olivia marveled at how blind men could be. Vesper might be a genius, but women and children were alien species to him. Gideon had been right. Hiding the formula with his family had made it nearly invisible to Lord Vesper.

"Your family is safe?" he asked, though he did not seem terribly concerned.

"Gone to the mainland," she said. "They could not bear the sight of these ruins. Or of *you*, my lord."

"Indeed? Leaving you all alone?"

"I'm sure they'll be back soon," she lied, "with the priest and the town elders and a good number of townsfolk. Gideon was well loved by your people."

Lord Vesper tensed, and Olivia knew he understood her meaning. Vesper might have many servants and allies around the world, but he was *not* well loved by his own people. If word began spreading that Vesper had a hand in Gideon's death, killing a man the peasants believed was a saint, working to free them from the plague . . .

"I see." Vesper backed up a step. He looked down at Gideon's body, and his nose wrinkled with distaste. Then he froze. Vesper had noticed the ring.

"A beautiful trinket," he mused. "It looks different somehow. . . ."

"A token of my love to Gideon," Olivia said as casually as she could manage. "An heirloom of my family."

"Will he be buried with it?"

Olivia felt the moment's importance, as if she were poised on the edge of a knife. Generations of Cahills — the future of the world itself — might be shaped by what she said and did next.

She tugged the ring off her husband's finger and thrust it toward Lord Vesper. "Do you want it, my lord? My wedding token to Gideon? Would you deprive me of that, too? Go on, then. Take it!"

Vesper's lip curled. He stepped away, immediately losing interest.

As Olivia had hoped: Anything freely given couldn't be worth much to a man like Damien Vesper. And a token of love? Worse than useless. He was a predator, a hunter by nature.

"There is no need to search the ruins," he decided. "Nothing could have survived."

"Because you were here when the laboratory exploded," Olivia guessed. "You saw it yourself."

Vesper smiled coldly. "We'll leave you to your grief, madam."

Olivia eased Gideon's head off her lap. She stood, clenching her fists. "You'll do more than that, my lord. You'll leave this island, and you'll never come back."

The guards frowned, obviously confused. Had a ragged, soot-covered woman just ordered Lord Vesper to leave?

"This is Cahill land," Olivia said. "Given by royal

charter. You are a guest here, but no longer. Leave now, my lord. I must bury my husband."

Vesper stared at her, his knuckles white on the pommel of his sword. Olivia met his eyes and let him know that she — a woman, a grieving wife and mother — was more dangerous right now than any weapon he could ever create. She would get her way, or she would destroy him.

One dangerous predator to another, Lord Vesper seemed to understand her. He nodded, his cold eyes boring into hers.

"Very well," he decided. "There is nothing left here worthy of my attention, at any rate. But, madam, I am still the lord of these lands. I will keep my eye on you and your family. If I find you have deceived me, if I come to suspect that you have hidden anything from me —"

"A widow and her children?" Olivia asked, feigning amazement. "How could we hide something from the eyes of Lord Vesper?"

Vesper wavered, perhaps catching a whiff of her sarcasm, but his pride won out. "Indeed," he muttered. "Remember me, madam. For I will remember you."

He turned and left, his guards falling in behind him.

Olivia did not relax until they reached the docks in the distance. She watched as the guards began preparing the lord's boat for crossing.

She turned to the ruins of her family house, the burned garden, and the dining table sitting in the fields, the only part of her old life left unscathed.

She looked down at her husband's pale face. No one would help her bury him, but she would manage. She would lay him to rest in the same graveyard where Cahills had been buried for generations.

Olivia might not be ladylike, young, or beautiful. She might not warrant a second look from a man like Lord Vesper, but she was strong. She could handle a shovel as well as a dagger or a cooking fire.

She slipped Gideon's gold ring on her finger, though it was much too big. She would need a chain to put it around her neck, she decided.

"I will keep it safe, Gideon," she promised. "Vesper will never have it."

Whatever Lord Vesper was hunting, he wouldn't succeed—not as long as Olivia Cahill drew breath. And she had a more important goal to keep her going. She must find a way to bring her children back.

"Some day, Gideon," she swore, "our family will sit again around this dining table. We *will* come together."

She glanced up as the morning sun illuminated the cliffs. Near the top was the cave where Gideon had proposed to her, and where Gideon's great ancestor, Madeleine the Matriarch, had surveyed the island and claimed it for her own.

Olivia rested her hand on her belly, though she could not feel the child kicking yet.

"I will name you Madeleine," she said. "You and

I will preserve this place and bring our family back together."

Olivia kissed her husband's golden ring. She would keep the ring a secret, next to her heart, for the rest of her life.

She must be strong. She needed no serum for that. She only needed her faith in her family. Someday, the Cahills would reunite. No one, not even Lord Damien Vesper, would stop her from succeeding.

She picked up a shovel from the garden and went to dig her husband's grave.

MADELEINE CAHILL
1526

As the last student fell unconscious to his desk, Madeleine Babbitt thought about lies.

She'd lived inside them all her life. Lies and secrets. Now she could shout out the truth, and no one would hear it. She smiled as she pulled a pencil from under the face of a slumped-over Flynn O'Halloran. His head thumped, echoing through the Xenophilus Institute of Alchemy, a grand name for a one-room schoolhouse made of clay and dried peat.

Maddy Babbitt, scared as a rabbit, they called her. She had acted the part almost all of her nineteen years. To keep attention away. To keep from being noticed. She almost believed she *was* that person. The stammer and the apologies had become part of her until her bolder side nearly faded away. Today, when Flynn had swiped her project notes and read them aloud, she had shrunk away. *A sleeping potion — aren't you boring enough?* he'd taunted. Everyone had dared her to demonstrate. So she had.

And it felt wonderful.

"Sleep well, my friends," she said, capping a vial of amber liquid. She glanced outside, looking for Professor Xenophilus, who had missed class today. A pity. He was probably lost in his own laboratory work, concocting medicines and marvelous inventions.

"As you only sniffed the potion on a handkerchief," she continued to the silent class, "you will waken in five minutes, fizzy and refreshed. Had it entered your bloodstream directly, it would take an hour."

Her stammer was gone. How liberating to speak to a stupefied audience! As she placed the vial into a pouch that hung around her neck, she felt fit to burst. Two decades of pent-up secrets bounced around inside her like unruly puppies before an opening door. "And also," she blurted out, "my name is not Maddy Babbitt! It's Madeleine . . ."

Say it! Go ahead.

But try as she might, the name *Cahill* stuck in her throat. Her training was bone deep.

As sunlight poked through the clouds and into the room, a tiny windmill of black-and-white sails began to turn on a table. These knocked a pebble down a chute, striking a hook that released a weighted pulley, which in turn raised a small spring-loaded hammer. The hammer then struck a brass gong, signifying the end of alchemy class.

Soon the distant tune would sound—Mother summoning her, expecting help in the apothecary.

Leaving behind the sleepers, Madeleine raced outside. She sped down a sloping path through heather and scrub. A low bank of clouds swept over the moor, casting the village of Scáth below in gray-green mist.

Madeleine looked up to the soft-ceilinged sky as she ran. She thought of her father, a man she'd never met. Mother claimed he had been the greatest alchemist and an even better father. She hoped that wherever he was, he was looking down and seeing the results of her alchemy training. Even more, she hoped he was proud.

In a moment, her shoes hit the cobblestones of town. She wove through winding alleys that echoed with the distant sound of a tin flute, piercing and sweet. This was Mother playing a tune called "Bhaile Anois," which meant *home now*. It was composed by Father and had become the traditional Cahill family song of summoning. As she ran, Madeleine waved to the pink-faced baker and soot-blackened chimney sweep, the burly butcher and weary lamplighter.

She dashed around the corner of Front Street. Carriages groaned up the hill, passing an old beggar woman who slept in the shadow of an abandoned stable. Ahead, the street descended toward the lake, where it flattened and followed the gentle curve of the bank. At the bottom of the hill stood O. Babbitt & Daughter Apothecary.

Madeleine slowed. Before the shop, a crowd of people had gathered in the street. A group of men was pounding on the front door. They were dressed in hooded capes of purple and black. Behind them stood a massive wooden dray cart tethered to pack horses. On the cart, three men lay moaning and half dead. Shackled to the cart's frame, his clothes ripped and face covered in blood, was Professor Xenophilus.

Madeleine stopped.

The old man slowly turned his gaze up the hill. His deadened eyes settled on her. He gestured feebly with an arm that hung at an odd, unnatural angle. *Run away*, his body language was saying.

One of the caped men spun toward Xenophilus, smacking his head with an open fist. The teacher's knees crumpled and he fell to the cobblestones. "Old fool," the man bellowed, "are ye sure there be Cahills here?"

Madeleine stumbled backward at the sound of the name she'd only ever heard uttered by her mother.

How did they know? How could Xenophilus—?

Last week. Under her teacher's observation she'd sampled an earlier version of the formula. Just a bit. Upon awakening, he'd scolded her about proper dosage. Too strong, and the potion induced coma! Ah, but too weak, and the recipient was half awake, unable to stop from saying his or her innermost thoughts!

The look on his face had startled Madeleine. His usual jovial, patient expression had changed. He seemed confused, as if seeing her for the first time.

I must have told him that day, she thought. *Under the earlier, weaker formula, I must have revealed my name.* It made sense—her father was so often on her mind.

Surely Xenophilus would have recognized the name of such a famous alchemist.

And now the secret had been beaten out of him—*because of me*, she thought. But by whom? Who were these people?

A loud crack rang out. The men were using a wooden ram now, and the apothecary door was about to give.

"We know you're in there, woman!" a voice shouted.

"Mother!" Madeleine screamed, running down the hill.

As she passed the stable, the beggar woman moved. Springing to her feet, she grasped Madeleine by the neck and dragged her into the shadows.

●●●●●

Over the years, Madeleine's training had included ancient fighting techniques to subdue men of great size and strength—but nothing for homeless old women in alleyways. "Let go, you old buzzard!" she cried, struggling against an iron grip.

As she whirled and lashed, the old lady countered every move. "Good grief, will you stop making such a racket!" she finally cried out. "They'll hear us!"

Madeleine froze in mid struggle. She fell to the ground and looked up into her adversary's face. *"Mother?"*

Olivia Cahill pulled back her woolen hood. "This old buzzard just saved your life," she said.

"I'm so sorry!" Madeleine protested.

Olivia put a gentle finger on her daughter's lips. "We must be quiet, and quick—"

Below them a voice boomed, loud and angry. *"Open in the name of Lord Vesper!"*

Vesper.

The name hit Madeleine like a shift in air pressure. As if the entire world were converging on her, pressing against her heart and brain. All her life, Damien Vesper had seemed more bogeyman than real—the shadow in the closet, the monster under the bed. *He will find us or die trying,* Mother had said. *And he will stop at nothing to get the secrets of the 39 Clues.*

Some monsters, Olivia had warned, were real. And to ward off this one, all Madeleine had needed to do was keep her mouth shut over the years.

One simple request, and she had failed.

"I-it's my f-f-fault, Mother!" Her stammer had returned with a vengeance. Madeleine felt the weight of her own betrayal. She had not only put Xenophilus's life in peril but exposed her and Olivia to their nemesis.

"Hush, darling daughter. It was only a matter of time. They have been trying for nearly two decades." Olivia's voice was parched. Reaching down into the folds of her ragged dress, she pulled out a small leather box. "Consider how lucky we are that we avoided them long enough for you to be prepared."

Prepared?

Madeleine felt anything but. Yes, for years she'd been learning the secrets of the 39 Clues, undergoing physical and mental training, tracking rumors about her siblings. Still, it had all seemed so . . . abstract. She had been born after the explosion that killed her father. She'd never met her brothers and sisters. Somehow, the Cahill saga seemed more legend than real, like the tale of the monster Vesper.

Another boom, like a cannon shot, echoed from down below.

Olivia flinched. "I had such hopes—we would outlast him, you would never face him in your lifetime. . . . But so be it. We will act quickly and decisively. Take this box—and please, recite for me your promises!"

Madeleine grabbed the box with shaky fingers. Mother had called this the Endgame Strategy. She hated the name. "B-b-but you will come, too, won't you?"

"He doesn't know you exist—so you must go forth alone, as planned. Your brothers and sisters are full of anger. They blame one another for your father's death. We will need to work on them. Be careful, and remember: Smartest always beats strongest. I will destroy what little is left of your father's work, and then I shall follow. Now, please, let me hear *the promises*. . . ."

Madeleine's mind raced, trying to remember. Father had a ring. It was an ugly thing, but it contained secrets. Secrets Olivia had never explained. *Keep Father's ring safe. That was Number One. Number Two was—*

Another sickening crack rent the air. A volley of triumphant voices.

The men were in.

Olivia stiffened. "I will go in the back way and hope they do not find the hidden door. Go!"

"But—the promises—" Madeleine protested.

"Just remember them, Madeleine, and whatever you do, stay alive. And one more thing. *Do not look back*." Tears in her eyes, Olivia cupped her daughter's face and planted a kiss on her cheek. "And may God go with you always!"

Before Madeleine could say another word, her mother was gone. Into the shadows and through a secret back door to the apothecary.

Madeleine stepped toward the door in pursuit. Her ear suddenly pinged with a high-pitched whoosh. She felt a trickle of blood down her neck. An arrow.

A finger's breadth to the left and it would have split her brain.

"You! Come out of the shadow!" a voice called up from below.

He doesn't know you exist.

There was work to be done. The Endgame was afoot.

Madeleine turned her back to the voice. Vesper could not see her face. She began to run, away from the stable, up the hill. She heard shouts and felt the zing of arrows all around her.

She heard another voice shout from below: "You imbecile, it's a lassie—too young for the wife! Spare my lord's arrows and help prepare the powder!"

Madeleine darted around the next corner. She knelt by the brick wall of the bakery and caught her breath. Blood had pooled in the well of her collarbone. Carefully, she touched the wound, but it seemed already to be healing.

The powder. What had he meant by—?

A sudden explosion rocked the stones beneath her feet. Inside the bakery, shock waves caused rolls and bread loaves to clatter to the floor.

As Madeleine scrambled to look around the corner, she heard a shriek that rose to an unearthly pitch and then ended in a guttural rattle.

The apothecary and the stable collapsed in a heap of brick and flames, with Olivia Cahill inside.

Madeleine could do nothing but scream.

●●●●●

1. *Keep the ring safe.*
2. *Never let anyone abuse the power of the 39 Clues.*
3. *Unite the Cahills when the time is right.*

The promises were stamped in Madeleine's brain. She hadn't recited them as her mother requested, and now they would not let her go. She drew her cloak against the bitter morning wind. Hidden behind a thick copse, she brushed away tears and glanced down through tangled, thorny branches.

In the village cemetery, a priest intoned prayers over a freshly dug grave.

Local merchants, arm in arm, wept for one of their own. The neighbors, many who owed their lives to

Olivia's healing skills, sobbed openly. Madeleine's friends clutched one another. So did her fellow apprentices, long recovered from the sleeping potion.

I am so, so sorry, Mother, she thought. But the unspoken words seemed hollow and pathetic.

She recalled Olivia's final two requests: *Stay alive. Do not look back.* Already Madeleine had broken the second one. Perhaps if she hadn't looked back, she wouldn't have seen the explosion. And all this would not have hurt so much.

Is this to be my fate? she thought. *To be a promise-breaker? A secret-revealer? A betrayer of the people I love most? A bringer of death?*

Madeleine could not stand the hiding. The fakery and failure. The idea that she had trained all her life for . . . *what*? What did any of it mean, now that her mother was dead?

She rose on unsteady legs. She would run down the hill, fling herself on the grave. She would beg God to return her mother and take her instead.

But her body went cold at the sight of a man on the edge of the gathering. His eyes were not focused on the service but instead scanned the countryside. He wore vestments of deep velvet and stood before a richly appointed carriage with magnificent horses. His face was lined and sagged with age, but he sported a mane of jet-black hair, save for a serpentine silver streak down the right side. And his expression made it clear he cared nothing for the deceased.

Vesper.

Madeleine remembered something her mother had said: *You will know Damien Vesper on sight, for he sucks the light from the sun.* She turned away, sick to the stomach. He had caused the deaths of both her parents. And she felt a crushing truth: The fate of the Cahills, the fate of the *world*, was solely between Vesper and . . .

Maddy Babbitt, scared as a rabbit.

Preposterous. Unthinkable.

Remember your training, she told herself. *The memorization, combat techniques, alchemy, survival exercises. The Endgame.* Try as she might, Madeleine could not think of herself as a warrior. She was who she was—a sheltered Irish country lass. She stood no chance alone against the forces of Lord Vesper.

It was over—the battle for the 39 Clues and all it stood for. Father's work had been destroyed. Even if Madeleine found her siblings, none knew the full secret of the formula. As for the ring—well, if Mother couldn't decode its message after two decades, Vesper would never do it, either. Running away was a fool's game. With his minions, Vesper would hunt her down like a wounded hare. Better to get it over quickly.

She stepped forward into the light.

Below her now, a bagpiper began playing the Cahill song, "Bhaile Anois." Madeleine's heart felt freshly bruised, as if Mother were rising before her. She could see Olivia's face in the frigid sky, smiling curiously. Madeleine wanted badly to talk to her. Her soul could not feel bleaker than this. She took a step forward, silently asking her mother for advice, forgiveness, and comfort.

As if in answer, a hint of a spring breeze whispered over the moor. It seemed to caress her face, to reach into her mind and lift a blanket from her memory. Her mother's words were as plain as if she were inches away. *Your father's mission was to heal. Vesper's is to control. He seeks the formula and suspects the secret of the ring. With the first, he will create a race of superhumans in his service. If he discovers the latter . . . woe betide the world, which will then be his.*

She fingered a bulge under her blouse. Overnight, while hiding in the academy, she had filched from storage a leather belt with a flat pouch. Into the pouch she had placed her sleeping potion vial and the contents of Mother's box: Gideon's mysterious gold ring. Olivia's handwritten notes about the possible whereabouts of Luke, Katherine, Thomas, and Jane. A small knife, a set of fishhooks, and hollow darts for hunting. A copy of the music to "Bhaile Anois." And a large sum of money.

No. Not the ring. Madeleine had taken it out last night. Just to examine, to try to make sense of the design. It was such a curious, odd-looking thing, with small ridges on the outer rim like cogs. She had placed it on her thumb and not yet taken it off! She turned from the funeral, pulling at the ring.

As the sun struggled through a gap in the clouds, the ring glinted. Madeleine quickly dropped it into her pouch. Stepping back behind the brush, she turned and ran.

Below her, Damien Vesper flinched at the sudden glare. And he looked up to see a figure disappearing into the heather.

●●●●●

"Nice, slimy baby," Master Winthrop Cahill said softly to the red-spotted newt in his hand. "Nice little lizard, who gets very, very scared of dark places . . ."

Threading his way through the crowded market, he was careful to avoid the throngs of buyers. Already he'd squashed a salamander and a tree toad.

Princess Mary Tudor was just ahead. As she walked, her horrid brown ringlets bounced, whisking the shoulders of her dress like little dancing brooms. Her legs were as spindly as twigs, and her shoulders heaved as she sniffled, which was almost all the time. Winthrop's father, Luke Cahill, said he was to marry her someday. Ha! He would rather live as a boil on the backside of a hairy boar. For one thing, she was only ten, a full year younger. For another, she was a first-class twit. Also, her nose ran faster than her bony legs, and she smelled of elderberries.

Not to mention she was ugly.

Mary held tight to the warty hand of their governess, Mistress Kletsch. With her other hand, Mistress Kletsch squeezed the merchants' fruits and vegetables while complaining about high prices. As if the king's governess needed to save money.

As Mary glanced over her shoulder, Master Winthrop cheerfully picked his nose and wiped it on a gooseberry. She crossed her eyes, stuck out her tongue, and turned away in disgust.

Now.

Lunging forward, he pulled back Mary's collar with one hand and dropped in the newt with the other. The creature's little eyes flashed with fright before it disappeared into the layers of fine silk and lace.

Princess Mary's shriek was sweet music.

Winthrop pretended to be examining a particularly interesting fig. "Is something wrong?" he said innocently. Watching the old lady fumble with the folds of clothing was even funnier than Mary's jerky dance.

"Master Winthrop Cahill, you lowborn pig, my father shall have your head!" the princess yelled.

But the boy's howls of laughter abruptly ended when the cart of figs and gooseberries came crashing down around him. "Thief! Thief!" a merchant cried out.

Princess Mary's screams were drowned out by voices shouting, "Over here!" and "Stop him!" As a gray-clad figure darted among the carts, a burly arm hurled a melon through the air. Apples went flying as people dove out of the way, running after the thief. Winthrop watched in awe. A humiliated Mary, a bandit in the market—could life possibly be sweeter?

He felt a reptilian claw closing over his arm. "Come

with me, young man," Mistress Kletsch commanded, pulling him back toward the carriage along with Princess Mary, who was now half undressed and weeping. The governess nearly threw them into the carriage, climbing in after them. "Go, Edward!" she cried.

The driver whipped the horses and the carriage took off. Crafted by King Henry VIII's master coachmaker, it raced smoothly over the English countryside away from the market. Mary and the governess were both yelling at Master Winthrop now, but all he wanted to do was look outside at the melee.

The carriage jounced abruptly. Winthrop's heart leaped with glee. Had they run over a dead body? Leaving Mary and the governess to their squealings, he looked out the back window. Alas, nothing to be seen but a dusty receding road.

Disappointed, he turned back. But not before catching a patch of gray wool just beneath the right corner of the window.

Curious, he climbed the seat again and gazed downward.

A pair of eyes gazed back up. The market thief was crouched on the carriage's running board, dressed in gray and wearing a woolen cap with a mask that covered all but his eyes. Clinging to a metal hook, he cast Master Winthrop a panicked, pleading look.

No. Not he. *She.* The thin physique, the long-lashed eyes made that clear.

More adventure! There was sure to be a reward for

this vagabond, and Edward the driver would revel in the capture.

Winthrop smiled at the thief and winked. *Don't worry,* he mouthed. Then he turned to the front of the carriage.

On his way to Edward, he took great care to step on the princess's foot. "Warty Winthrop!" she cried out.

"Bloody Mary!" he spat back.

The carriage jounced again. Master Winthrop spun around. He looked out the back of the carriage just in time to see the thief running off down the road. And he watched carefully as she stuffed something into the knot of a gnarled oak tree, whose arms looked like those of a wild dancer.

•••••

"Wicked, wicked, *wicked* child!" said old Williams, dragging Master Cahill by the arm though the Persian rug–covered corridors of King Henry VIII's Palace of Placentia.

"Last time it was four *wicked*s and one *wretched*," Master Winthrop chirped. "*Incorrigible*, too. Whatever that means."

Williams tut-tutted, yanking the boy around a marble-columned corner. "What on earth have you done to make dear, gentle old Mistress Kletsch resign? The fifth governess in three months! How can we expect to replace her on such short—*where is Hargrove*? Hargrove promised he would meet us with another candidate for the king's approval!"

"Mistress Kletsch smells like the fart of a dying wart-hog," Winthrop replied. "And that's after she has taken a bath."

"Dastardly boy—foul, odious boy!" Williams said, looking around frantically for his fellow courtier.

"Odious . . ." Winthrop said. "I like that."

Stepping into the opening of the king's chamber, Williams was suddenly calm and ramrod straight. He held Winthrop tightly to his side, set his face into a neutral expression, and cleared his throat. "Ahem."

Standing next to King Henry was a man with massive shoulders, fierce eyes, and long black hair. As he paced before a line of prisoners, his cape billowed around his gray robe. He was staring at the first man in line, a broad, curly-haired fellow with few teeth and soiled hands.

Winthrop loved watching his father at work.

"You say you did not steal the sheep from your lord, then?" said Luke Cahill, his voice a deep, rasping snarl. "You say you are a vegetable farmer?"

The man quivered as he replied. "Yes, milord. Them foxes is bedevilin' the countryside a-nights, and they eats the sheeps, they does."

"Ah, true, true," Luke said, pacing a circle around the man. "No doubt you were home at the time of the thefts, tending to your lessons in proper speaking and good grammar."

Master Winthrop let out a guffaw that was stifled by Williams's gnarled, powder-scented hand.

Spinning around, Luke swiftly took the prisoner's hand and rubbed it on his own face. "If these are the hands of a vegetable farmer," he said, holding the man's hands toward the king, "then what explains the scent of grease that is now on my face—sheep-wool grease?"

The farmer's jaw flapped, his eyes desperate. "But—but I—"

"Ha! Brilliant, Cahill!" the king bellowed, applauding lustily. "Good, then, behead the lout."

The man fell to his knees in tears. "Milord? I has me a fambly, five little boys and a wife what's with child. Hunger is to blame, not deviltry! I beg you, spare me!"

"Five boys?" King Henry's smile fell and his eyes began to moisten. Master Winthrop had seen this reaction before. The king wanted a son more than anything. Thus far, his only offspring was Mary. According to the so-called Rules of Succession, a daughter was not guaranteed to inherit the throne. But the son of a king automatically became king. Henry had grown so frustrated, he had begun blaming his wife, Catherine, the daughter of the Spanish king and queen. Henry claimed she was cursed. He was trying to convince the pope to annul the marriage. Now he had his eye on a woman named Anne Boleyn—perhaps if they married, *she* would give him a son! "Not one boy, but five . . ." the king said softly to the farmer. "You are a lucky man. And we are not without mercy. I sentence you to . . . oh, three days in the stockade!"

The man's face broke into a grateful smile. He shouted thanks as guards whisked him away. "I daresay I have a soft heart, Cahill," the king murmured. "I wish these men feared me as much as they do my adviser!"

"What some call weakness others recognize as wisdom, my lord," Luke said, bowing to the king. "And now, a moment's pardon while I tend to my son."

"Yes, yes, of course." The king waved him away, plucking grapes from a gilded plate.

As Luke loped toward the door, Williams began to shake with fear. "Lord Cahill," he said, holding out a parchment scroll, "we have received a formal resignation from yet another—"

Luke batted the parchment away. "Are you so poorly suited, Williams, to the task of finding one good governess from among the entire population of England?"

Williams bowed, blathering apologies. But Luke pulled his son into the corridor. "What now?" he scolded. "You are expected to shine before the king!"

"So I can marry his wretched daughter?" Master Winthrop mumbled.

"Who will give birth someday to an heir," Luke said, "who will then be king. A *Cahill* king! Don't you see? The daughter will not necessarily earn the throne. But whomever she *marries* shall become king!"

"Does that seem fair, Father?" Winthrop asked.

"Fair?" Luke drew his son closer, his face growing red. "Is it fair to watch one's father burned to death and be blamed for his murder? Is it fair when sickness takes one's beloved? Is it fair to wander the countryside destitute, with a baby boy? I worked my way into this court by grit and cunning. I had to step over others who wanted it less. Fairness was not part of the calculation. My only desire is to redeem our family. House of Lancaster, House of York, House of Tudor—*pah*! It will be the dawn of the Lucian Age."

Master Winthrop frowned. He had heard this story too many times. What was so great about being king anyway? Better to be a bandit or a jousting knight! "But, Father, the king wants to divorce Queen Catherine," Master Winthrop pressed on. "Then Mary will no longer be princess. And then I will have to be married to that hideous —"

"Mary will remain princess," his father snapped. "And you will be closest in line for the throne. I shall make that certain."

"But there are others in line to succeed—"

"Not to worry, Luke; I have plans for the others."

Master Winthrop shuddered. His father's tone of voice suggested something far worse than pranks with salamanders.

He tried not to think of the word *assassination*.

"My lord?" a voice piped up from behind them.

The two Cahills turned. Hargrove, the king's man-servant, was standing in the corridor with a young woman in a peasant dress and governess's bonnet, her face cast toward the floor. "I would like to introduce a candidate for the office of governess, a fine young woman of exceeding—"

"Yes, yes," Luke said impatiently, "surely she can speak for herself. Is the floor about to collapse, girl, is that why you look down? Do you have a name?"

Master Winthrop was used to people's reactions upon meeting his father. Some cried. Others shrank away. Two or three had even fainted, such was his power. But he had never seen an expression like this young woman's. Her eyes fixed on Luke's intently, as if she were trying to look through them to the other side of his head. Then they softened, misted over, as if she were about to cry—but not with fear, exactly. With some other kind of emotion Winthrop couldn't name. If it didn't seem so absurd, he'd think it was something like joy.

"I am M-M-Madeleine Babbitt," she said, "of Scáth."

"A daughter of Ireland, then," Luke grunted, his own brogue sneaking into his speech. "Well, let's hope this one lasts longer than a week."

As he walked back into the chamber, Master Winthrop stared coldly at the new governess. He didn't like her. She was too young and too strange. She had no warts or whiskers. And she didn't smell bad. What fun was that?

"I'm sure we will become close friends," said the Irish lass.

Master Winthrop crossed his eyes, said "close friends" with a lisp, and stalked away.

But he couldn't help noticing that her face seemed very familiar.

⦁⦁⦁⦁⦁

Madeleine Cahill shivered. She had lived through nineteen frigid winters by the lake, but nothing prepared her for the iciness of her brother Luke.

She paced her spare, dank bedchamber — seven steps from one end to the other. The height of English power, and all they could give her were four stone walls, a dusty wood floor, and a bed with a sunken horsehair mattress!

Her eyes kept darting toward the window. Every flash of white gave her a start.

Vesper had been in the food market. She'd seen his badger-head of hair. If she hadn't caused the distraction by upsetting the fruit cart, he might have caught her. How long could she keep this up? How long could she survive alone? She would have to confront Luke, get him to join her. Somehow.

She had come too far to fail. On the days following the funeral she'd become ill in the forest. Overcome by cold, rain, grief, and self-doubt, she had nearly died. But as she read her mother's notes by a peat fire, one line had struck her:

Luke: stable hand, H VIII

H VIII meant King Henry the Eighth. The Palace of Placentia was just outside London. A huge journey—across the Irish Sea, all of Wales, and most of England! But Luke seemed her best hope. He was twenty-three years older than Madeleine. He would be the wisest sibling. So she'd mastered disguises, stowed away on a trade ship, slept in caves and trees—somehow managing to leave each location just as Vesper arrived to try to flush her out. By the time she reached London, she'd nearly starved. Seeing the ROYAL GOVERNESS WANTED notice had been a stroke of luck.

Royal Governess Wanted

For Service in His Majesty's Household

Apply to Mr. Hargrove, Palace of Placentia

And now . . . what? How much better was her brother than her enemy?

Olivia had once described Luke as "larger than life" and "forceful." But this man was also bloodless, cruel, and deeply sad. His eyes seemed to be following Madeleine still, hovering, judging, condemning. They were nearly the same eyes as her mother's, piercing and smart—but with all the kindness drained out. Like a familiar painting with one color removed.

Madeleine thought about Promise Three: *Unite the Cahills when the time is right*. Was the time right? Was Luke ready to give up his place in the court to help unite the family?

His eyes didn't seem to hint at yes.

Outside her window, she could see knights practicing for a joust. On a vast field they raced their horses at top speed, thwacking targets made of pigskin stuffed with straw. One of the knights, who rode a majestic dun-colored horse, had far more power and agility than the others. She watched as he came to rest and took off his helmet.

She was not completely surprised to see it was the king himself, Henry VIII. He was known as a champion jouster. But even he, the most powerful man in Great Britain, feared her brother Luke.

In moments, young Master Winthrop would be arriving for his first lesson, and she needed to prepare. Williams had suggested tin flute lessons, "a taming influence for the little beast."

Madeleine looked forward to that. Olivia had taught her to play. *You've a jot of Jane in you*, Mother would say after a particularly fine lesson. Madeleine cherished

that comment. There were other compliments, too—
a cut of Katherine, a touch of Thomas, a lick of Luke—for
her technical skills, athletic victories, strategic thinking. She was a bit like them all, Olivia had said, but
with an extra quality all her own. *Do not let the meekness
swallow you, Madeleine, for someday people will see you for
who you are. You are strong yet with the soul of a peace-
maker. You bring people together. Call it a magnificence of
Madeleine.*

She hadn't been feeling very magnificent lately.
But with a roof over her head and food in her belly,
she could think clearly now. And plan. She would win
over Winthrop first. Work her way into Luke's trust.
And when she felt comfortable, she would reveal her
identity. That would be the "right time" to begin fulfill-
ing Olivia's dream.

A united Cahill family.

Madeleine picked up the tin flute and played a bit.
The instrument was rusted and sounded like a dying
weasel. She suspected there was a hole and found one
at the bottom of the instrument. She looked around for
something to plug it. Horsehair? Too flimsy. A ripped
piece of fabric? Too bulky.

She checked the hallway—empty. Reaching under
her blouse she unhooked the pouch and peered inside.
Hooks and darts? The wrong shape.

Then she held up the ring.

The flute tapered to a tip narrow enough to slip the

ring over. Carefully, she slid it up the instrument. It fit snugly over the hole, as if it were meant to be there.

Madeleine played a C major scale, which floated through the room, clear and sweet. She smiled. If only she could afford to expose the ring like this! Naturally, that was impossible. It would be violating Olivia's promise.

Or would it?

Professor Xenophilus liked to say that the best hiding places were in plain sight. Only Mother and Father knew about the ring. Vesper was chasing her for the serum formula and knew nothing about the ring. If Madeleine were to be captured, it would make sense for the ring *not* to be on her anyway. . . .

A loud burp at the door made her jump. She turned to face her scowling charge, who stared at her with folded arms.

If you let him control you, Williams had warned, *you will lose both this job and your sanity.* "You are seven minutes late," Madeleine said. "I trust that will not happen again—"

"I know who you are," the boy interrupted.

Madeleine's heart began to pound. Had she been followed? Had Luke recognized her? "Kn-kn-know me?" she said.

"You're the thief!" Master Winthrop blurted out triumphantly. "From the market! I saw you on the back of the royal carriage, with a mask!"

Relief washed over Madeleine. Dealing with a mischievous child was one task she was sure she could handle. "Well. I guess you've flushed me out. . . ."

"Like a pheasant!" Winthrop crowed. Hands on hips, head cocked, he began circling Madeleine. "But we are not without mercy. I will spare you, but I have some demands." He began counting off demands on his stubby fingers. "Five minutes of memorization per week. Latin only on Tuesdays. No mathematics ever. Three hours for lunch. Vegetables forbidden. I eat and drink what I want. And no wooden paddle."

"You are a clever negotiatior," Madeleine said.

"I am the son of Luke Cahill." Master Winthrop preened as he sat on the edge of the bed. "And I have decided that I shall not learn today."

"Oh?" Madeleine nodded. "Well, then, fine."

"Because I have too much gas, and the flute will make me . . ." Winthrop's voice trailed off. "Did you say . . . 'fine'?"

"This hour belongs to you. If you choose not to learn, then I will play and you can listen."

She lifted the tin flute to her mouth. He looked away, already bored. Eyeing the ring, Madeleine realized it resembled no more than a grooved collar. With its cogged design, it could have been found on the floor of the smithy's shop. No one would take it for a valuable secret. And it certainly made the flute sound magnificent.

As she played a country air, Master Winthrop's expression began to soften. His body swayed when she followed with a sad ballad. Before long, he and Madeleine were dancing to an Irish reel, both of them collapsing with laughter on the bed.

"Well," Madeleine said finally. "Shall we move on to a history lesson?"

"No!" Winthrop snapped, grabbing the tin flute. "Teach me!"

She raised an eyebrow.

He smiled meekly. "Please?"

•••••

Who would have thought Master Winthrop had a jot of Jane?

To Madeleine's surprise, he was a wonderful musician, a natural. Which played right into her plan. She would stage a recital. Luke could not help but be impressed with her skills as a governess!

One week later she stood before the king, Luke, and assorted courtiers.

"M-may I have your attention, lords and l-ladies." Madeleine shook as she looked around the music chamber. She eyed the tin flute. Gideon's ring still covered the hole. In a fit of nervousness, she had tried to remove it, but Master Winthrop had screamed at her. He'd claimed the flute sounded "odious" without it. And young Winthrop did not take no for an answer. "We h-h-have a very s-s-special musical p-p-performer—" she continued.

Master Winthrop yawned loudly, twirling the tin flute. Madeleine prayed the ring stayed on. She vowed to remain calm about it. After the recital, the king would surely allow the court to buy a new tin flute. And she would pocket the ring again. "M-may I p-present the very talented Master Winthrop Cahill!" she declared.

The king clapped his beefy hands.

As Winthrop began playing, Henry VIII smiled sleepily. Luke stared at his son with intensity.

What is he feeling? Madeleine couldn't tell. Luke looked at everything the same way. Like a viper eyeing its prey.

As the recital ended, the king shouted, "Bravo, boy! Excellent!" Master Winthrop took a bow, and another, and another.

By then, even Luke was smiling. The expression softened his face, made him look more Cahillian than ever. But as the court all gathered to praise the boy, no one said a word to Madeleine. Not even a curt "thank you." Not even Luke.

She bowed, exited the room, and sat on a banquette in the corridor, waiting for Master Winthrop to emerge. This was not what she had planned.

She was a nobody here. To break through to her brother, she needed to be a *presence*. She closed her eyes, trying to picture Olivia's face. *Guide me,* she thought.

A moment later, a gangly, sooty-faced young man came skittering down the hall. He leaned toward

Madeleine, panting. His breath smelled of goose liver. "Bobbitt?" he said, sending a rotten blast that nearly made her gag.

"Please keep a gentlemanly distance," Madeleine said. "And it's Babbitt."

"Oh. Right." He lurched forward, taking her by the arm.

"I beg your pardon!" Madeleine cried. "Unhand me or I will call for Luke Cahill."

The man grinned and tightened his grip. "The Lord Luke's what sent for me! I'm under personal orders to escort Madeleine Bobbitt meself!"

"Escort?" Madeleine said. "Where?"

"Where do you fink, mum? The royal counting-'ouse?" The man laughed hysterically. "Come along — you are under arrest!"

⬤⬤⬤⬤⬤

Madeleine hadn't expected King Henry's prison to be so like her maid's quarters. The big difference was the metal bars, the unearthly stench, and the granite bench that numbed her rear end.

Why?

No one had given her an explanation for being here. She could barely understand the guard's accent. Was it something Master Winthrop had told them, some dreadful lie?

It took her hours to fall asleep against the cold stone. She dreamed longingly about the horsehair bed.

The voice of Luke Cahill jarred her awake. "Well, who knew my little boy had such a gift for music?" he rasped in the darkness. "My compliments on the tutoring."

Madeleine sat up with a start. She shivered as his silhouette drew closer, lit from behind by the guard's lantern. Dressed in a full-length fur coat, he resembled some kind of ghoulish beast, half man and half bear. The day's events rushed over her—the bruises, the unfairness. "This s-s-seems an unlikely form of g-g-gratitude."

Luke sat next to her, his features inches away yet mere shadowy blots in the darkness. "Well, then, you will no doubt have a satisfactory answer to this question: Where did you get the ring?"

She felt the blood draining from her face. "You—you know about it?"

"My father wore it every day. I would tease him about it. Such a crude thing. It was one of a kind, he said. That was all." Luke leaned closer. "He died in a fire. Everything he had—his clothing, his jewelry, his life's work—destroyed. And yet, his ring appears *on a tin flute.*"

As Maddy Babbitt shrank in fear, Madeleine Cahill sized up her brother. She had to remain calm. To follow through in her plan despite the setback. "May I see the ring?" she asked.

"Do you think I would be so idiotic as to have it with me?" Luke snapped. "Perhaps you can begin by telling me who you are, and why you had it!"

Madeleine's heart sank. He had probably put it in a safe place, or given it to one of his trusted courtiers. They all lived in fear of him and would do whatever he asked. He was too cagey to carry it around.

Which meant that Promise Number One—*Keep the ring safe*—had been broken.

Her only hope was to force Promise Number Three.

She could no longer wait to win his trust. She had to reveal her identity. The reuniting of the Cahills must begin. Now.

"B-b-before you fled," she said carefully, "your mother had neglected to mention something about her c-c-condition."

Even in the dim light, Madeleine could see the knife-sharpness of his glare. "I will listen to you for precisely one minute. I advise you—no nonsense."

"Luke . . ." Madeleine took a deep breath. "My name isn't Babbitt. Mother was with child on the last day you saw her. I was that baby."

Luke did not move for a good twenty seconds. She tried to read the expression on his face but couldn't. Then, slowly, he reached out and cupped her chin gently in his hand, moving her face right and left.

"'Swounds . . ." he said. "Good grief, yes . . . the resemblance . . ."

This close, she could see the icy veil over his eyes disappear, as if Olivia herself were peering through. In a flash, Madeleine sensed that her long trip—through fear and sickness, disguises and lies—hadn't been a waste after all.

She wanted to throw her arms around him. But it was too early for that. The bond was new and fragile. One step at a time. As tears streamed down her cheeks, she felt herself laughing, overcome with joy and relief. "I—I have so much to tell, my brother."

"I know you do." Luke took her hand and stood.

Where to begin? She would save the sad news of Mother's death till the end. There were nearly two decades of catching up. "Mother and I . . . we were living in exile. Under invented names. Babbitt—can you imagine? Not even a name with a bit of . . . *flash*, such as, I don't know, Ravenwood. Or Lancelot! I had to become quiet, to deflect attention. Like a scared little mouse! Anyway, Mother secretly trained me all my life for this final mission—"

"Shhh, my dear," Luke said. "Please. Don't rush. It is an emotional moment, I can see. I will give you time to put together your feelings and your story. But if it comforts you any, please know I have heard it all already."

Madeleine wiped a tear. "You *have?*"

"Oh, yes, many times." Luke chuckled. "The details are different, but the broad story is the same."

"I—I'm afraid I don't understand . . ." Madeleine stammered.

Luke stood at the door, signaling the guard to open it. "I daresay you're far more talented than the last one who claimed to be a sibling. My long-lost brother Nigel—lived in hiding under a false identity and so forth. And before him was sister Gladys, aunt Puff, and cousin Quincy—"

"But—there is no Nigel Cahill, or any of the others!"

"Or Maddy Cahill!" Luke's voice was more of a slap than a sound. "Why did you display the ring? What on earth is your plan?"

"I did it to p-p-plug a hole!"

Luke turned in disgust. "No matter. If you have other agents in this palace, they will be routed. If you have thought to flush me out by the sight of this ring—if you are planning an ambush—your people will find nothing on me. Before long, your employer will know that after all these years, his plans have failed. And revenge will follow."

"Employer?" Madeleine shrank back into the cell. She wasn't understanding a word of his rant.

"Do not take me for a fool. Only one person could have had possession of this ring. The one who watched my father die. The one whose blindness and greed have just ensured his own defeat." Luke turned to the guard. "Simon, prepare the prisoner for public execution in two days. Send an invitation far and wide, and be on the lookout for a man named Vesper."

"Vesper?" Madeleine said. "How can you possibly think—?"

"I shall send for the hangman right away!" Simon replied.

"Not a hanging," Luke replied with a slow smile. "I would prefer a slow burning at the stake, and a front-row seat."

•••••

"CCCHHHH . . . HELP!"

At the noise, Simon fell off his chair, ending a blissful dream. "Whaa? *Szzzzm?* Oh, for the love of 'Enry . . ."

The choking was from the new prisoner. The young girl. Bobbitt. The spy. He shook himself awake and rose.

Lighting a lantern, he approached the cell. "Wha' then?" he called out. "Roast pheasant caught in yer froat?"

He snickered. The prisoners always liked a bit of humor.

But the choking now sounded like vomiting, which made the guard blanch. Last time that happened, the prisoner died before he could have a proper beheading. And there went an honest day's pay. "'Old yer puke, will ye, and I'll fetch somefing to drink."

He returned to his station, a hard seat by the hallway wall. On the floor was a chamber pot, a spittoon, and a jug of cheap beer he'd been sipping for hours. All day long he'd been confusing them. "S'pose it don't matter which . . ." he murmured to himself with a chuckle.

The jug of beer smelled a bit off, but he brought it down the hallway and fumbled with the key. "'Elp is 'ere!" he said, opening the gate.

Simon felt a tiny sting in his neck. And all went black.

●●●

Madeleine tiptoed past the guard. He was fast asleep.

She managed a smile. The sleeping potion had worked, and the dart had held just enough of it to knock him out.

"*I enjoy rainy days . . .*" Simon said. "*And I miss my little doggie. . . .*"

Madeleine realized the dose must have been a bit too weak. *Too little, and the victim will begin revealing his innermost thoughts,* Professor Xenophilus had said.

This meant she didn't have long to make her escape. Maybe fifteen minutes.

In the darkness, she had managed to change clothes. Simon's uniform was filthy and far too large for her frame. She couldn't do much about the aroma, but at least the hooks from Olivia's secret pouch held the material together adequately.

As she began climbing a set of steep stone steps, Simon was confessing his fear of bunny rabbits. He would be awake soon, but the fact that he was wearing a governess's dress meant he might not call for help quite so quickly.

She tried to look on the bright side. But the ring was lost, Luke thought she was Vesper's spy, and if she were caught, she would die. Her best hope was escape, from one of the most heavily guarded palaces in the world.

She had made stupid, unforgivable mistakes. Putting the ring on the tin flute. Allowing Master Winthrop to convince her to keep it there. Expecting that no one would recognize it.

As she neared the top of the stairs, she made a vow.

She would escape and regroup. She would use every ounce of her skill and cunning to find the ring. Somehow. And when she did, she would never let anyone, or anything, block the fulfillment of the promises.

From this point on, if she survived, the plan would be radically different. It would involve infinite patience. Observation. And more patience. If it took her lifetime—her children's lifetime, *their* children's—if it took the creation of a secret family *within* the family, so be it. The 39 Clues would remain secret for centuries if necessary. Until the moment when the families were ready to unite.

From this point on, Maddy Babbitt was dead.

Long live Madeleine Cahill.

At the landing, she inserted a large skeleton key into the thick, brass-plated wooden door. It creaked loudly as it opened.

"Wha? Hrrrrumph!" a gruff voice shouted. Another guard.

Madeleine's legs locked. She cleared her throat and lowered her voice as far as it would go. "Go back to s-s-sleep," she grumbled.

"Right, then, Grandmother . . ." came the answer, followed by a snore.

She stepped out into a narrow hallway. It led past a row of small warrenlike rooms, the living quarters for the kitchen maids. They were already awake, baking and preparing the day's meals. As Madeleine darted past the kitchen, the scent of warm bread made her mouth water.

She followed candle-lit sconces through a long corridor. The palace was a maze, but at some point, if she walked far enough, she'd reach a door. She grabbed one of the sconces and held it like a torch.

"I beg your pardon?" a voice called from behind her. "May I ask what business you have here?"

It was Williams, the boy's valet.

Madeleine's mind raced. Luke had said he did not have the ring. Which meant he had given it to someone he trusted. Could it be Williams? "Hrrrm . . . Lord Cahill has sent me to fetch the ring," she said in her guard voice.

"Ah, the ring, yes," Williams said. "And you have the written request, do you?"

"Erm, yes, of course," Madeleine said. She reached inside the shirt for her pouch. For the darts.

Williams was backing away. Suddenly he shouted, "Holworthy! Wigglesworth! Stoughton! *Hargrove!*"

Change of plans. Madeleine charged forward, sending Williams sprawling into the hall. To her left, an older man in a plaid nightgown and tasseled sleeping cap appeared in a doorway. *"Guard!"* he shouted. *"We have an impostor in the palace!"*

Madeleine raced the other way, ducking to the left down another long, straight section of the hallway. At the end of it was a square of dull amber light. The sun was beginning to rise. Soon the entire palace would be awake.

The hallway ended in a T, and men were approaching from either side. She wheeled around. The old man was padding toward her, followed by a gaggle of butlers and scullery maids brandishing wire whisks and serving spoons. There was nowhere to go.

Except one.

She leaned back, pushed open the window, and jumped.

•••••

Goat manure, though no one's favorite substance, had the benefit of being soft. As Madeleine sprang to her feet, she wondered just how many more charms of King Henry's court she would discover.

She had landed at the edge of the royal garden. Above her, the palace rang with commotion. She raced toward a barn. Ducking around a corner, she nearly fell into a large barrel.

Rainwater.

She continued her course into the barrel, feetfirst. The water's color clouded fast, and when she jumped out she felt a bit more pleasant, and less fragrant. By now she could hear people running across the farm toward her. She headed toward the open barn door.

An ox-drawn cart emerged, laden with hay bales. The ox driver was gazing curiously toward the commotion, away from Madeleine. She dove onto the cart, nestling herself between bales.

The cart's wheels creaked loudly beneath her as they moved. She peered out from the hay. In the distance, the sun struggled over the horizon, casting the grounds in a silvery predawn glow. One by one, darkened palace windows were flickering with light. A small arched door flew open, and someone rushed out, dressed in a servant's black cloak. She squinted, trying to recognize the face before the figure rushed away toward the livery stable.

Hargrove. Heading in the wrong direction.

The cart was slowing now. From behind her, she heard the breathless voice of a guard grilling the driver. She didn't hear the questions exactly, but she heard the driver's annoyed reply: "Wha' kind of palace is it where ye can't keep track of yer own governesses? *You* skitter about after 'er, mate. I gots me work to do."

Thank you, she thought, staying still as the cart trundled to who-knew-where. She was too afraid to poke her head up, but she finally did when the cart eventually came to a stop.

She recognized the destination. The jousting field. A few yards to the right was a large wooden shed where the knights prepared for practices. It was quiet now, and inside there was sure to be another change of clothes—dry and hayless.

As the driver began discussing the weather with someone, Madeleine slipped off the cart and into the shed. Hay stuck to every inch of her. A sleeping stable boy opened his eyes briefly and went back to sleep. In the morning light, Madeleine saw suits of metal armor, chain mail, pads, boots, helmets, full-body undergarments, saddles, stirrups, curry combs, tack of all sorts, swords, lances, maces, and weapons she couldn't name. But she was most interested in the undergarments, some of which looked boy size. Quickly she changed into one, a black fabric suit that fit perfectly. It felt good to be dressed in something clean.

Tethered to a pole at one end of the shed were two flea-bitten horses, suited up and ready for the day's jousting. They gazed lazily at her, then went back to chewing a meager scattering of hay.

"'Ungry, mates?" came the driver's voice, just outside the door. "'Igh quality 'ay, comin' yer way—and dry 's a bone!"

Madeleine panicked. No one in the kingdom would fail to recognize a young woman in men's garments.

● ● ●

"Saints alive, ain't they feedin' yer nothin' but crickets and mice?" the driver said as he entered, letting a bale of hay slip from each shoulder before the grateful horses. Outside, the king's men were jabbering on about the missing governess.

"'Ear that? Missing lassie! Meself, I don't blame 'er. That Master Winthrop is worse than a stubborn nag—no offense." He slipped the horses a couple of sugar cubes before exiting. "'Ere, put some fat on yer spindly bones."

Madeleine watched it all through the slits of a helmet. She hadn't imagined how heavy a helmet and a suit of chain mail could be. Or how hot. Or what a perfect hiding place it was.

By the time the voices began to recede, she felt like she was roasting. Through the slits in the helmet she could see the stable boy stirring. She would have to gain his trust. She lifted one leg and stepped forward. The chain mail clanked heavily. "Please," she said, her voice sounding dull and muffled through the helmet, "wake up."

The boy's eyes flickered open and he sprang to his feet. "I'm—I'm sorry," he cried out. "I worked through the night, I did. Only been sleepin' a moment or two—"

Before Madeleine could reply, a deep voice thundered from the open door. "Good morrow, McGarrigle! Are we ready?"

"Er . . . almost, my lord," the boy replied.

Madeleine turned. Ducking through the door was an older man, holding a riding crop. Glancing at Madeleine, he grinned. "Well, I'll be a two-headed buzzard— 'tisn't often that a jousting partner arrives this early.

Fearless fellow, eh? Let me know when ye're in yer tournament armor, and we can begin straight away. Make sure this man has a fine mount, McGarrigle!"

Madeleine could feel her chain mail clatter as she shook. "Mount?" she said in her deepest voice to McGarrigle. "As in . . . *mount*?"

"It won't be so bad," the boy said, approaching her with a heavy set of metal armor, "as long as ye're protected wiff these."

It took about twenty minutes for Madeleine to climb into the armor, with the boy's help. It felt as if she were wearing a small building. "I'm supposed to move in this?" she asked.

"It's the least 'eavy suit we 'ave." The boy, who was examining the teeth of the two horses, took the reins of one and brought it closer. "This old nag may stay on its feet for a few moments at least," he said. "Good luck jousting wiff the old fellow."

"But—" Madeleine said.

"Step on this," McGarrigle said, pushing her onto a wooden platform, which he raised with a massive winch.

Madeleine felt herself rising in jolts of motion until her knees were the height of the horse's back. With a swift move, McGarrigle slid her leg off the platform and out over the horse. She landed on the horse's back with a thud, causing its knees to buckle.

"Sorry, I has to do this wiff all his partners," McGarrigle said, adding with a rueful sigh, "but never the same feller twice, if ye know what I mean."

Madeleine felt the blood drain from her face. "Let me down!" she protested. But McGarrigle thrust into her hand a lance that felt as heavy as a tree, and her shoulder was nearly wrenched out of its socket.

"We'll share a cup afterward," the boy said, "if yer head's still attached."

"Wait—this is a m-m-mistake!" Madeleine stammered, lifting her visor.

"You bet yer sweet buzzard it is," the boy said, giving the horse a good, hard kick.

Madeleine's visor slammed shut as the horse galloped into the sunlight. She fought to stay upright, to keep her lance from drooping to the ground.

The field was long and dusty, with a few rows of empty seats on either side. At the far end, her opponent sat tall atop a black steed whose leg muscles bulged and glistened. "Ah, grand!" he shouted, clutching his helmet to his side. "It's not often the Spanish ambassador arrives early for a joust. I was expecting not to see you at all!"

Spanish ambassador?

Madeleine recognized the voice before she could see him through the slits of her visor. It was King Henry.

In his armor, he appeared to be the size of two men. He handled his own lance as if it were a willow wisp. With a grin, he raised the visor of his helmet. "I have received word of your . . . disapproval of my desire to annul my marriage. You know my position, and you know my right as king. Yet still you protest. Perhaps we shall decide this matter on the field?"

Madeleine tried to think of something to say, but it was enough just to keep upright. Out of the corner of her eye, she spotted a distant fancy carriage approaching — probably the *real* ambassador.

"I take your silence as an agreement!" the king bellowed, lowering the visor. His horse dipped its head twice, impatiently striking the ground with its hooves. As steam puffed from its nostrils, it looked more bull than horse.

"Readyyyyyy!" King Henry called out, raising his lance high.

I'm dead, Madeleine thought.

If he even so much as swung that lance, its wind alone would knock her over. She had to get away. Now.

"About f-f-ace!" she said to the horse, flailing with her boots. "Into the barn, please. It's time for some tasty hay! *Haaaaaaay!*"

The horse took off like a shot, toward King Henry. The king seemed surprised, as if he wasn't expecting her to go just yet. "Cheating does not work in England," he hissed.

He kicked his horse. The steed dug in hard, sending up storm clouds of dirt. The king's eyes blazed through the visor as he slowly lowered the lance.

It was pointed at Madeleine's heart.

No time to think. She lifted her lance, too, but it was far too heavy. Even if she could strike him, the torque alone would pull her off the horse.

King Henry was forty yards away . . . twenty . . .

Madeleine's shoulder was falling. The tip of the lance was nearly to the ground. And her horse was headed directly *at* King Henry instead of to his side.

"Blast it, what are you doing?" he cried.

Remember, smartest always beats strongest.

Olivia's words were like a trumpet call. Madeleine ungritted her teeth and let out a scream.

The tip of her lance dug into the soil. It bent into a taut C. She felt her body lifting out of the saddle. She pulled back on her boots, releasing them from the stirrup. Freeing her from the horse.

The weight of her suit almost broke the lance, but instead she vaulted high into the air.

From below her came a bloodthirsty yell. She felt the whoosh of King Henry's lance as it passed beneath her feet and over the top of her horse's saddle. Her lance twanged as it grazed the royal steed's flank. She held tight. As the pole retracted and straightened, for a moment Madeleine was suspended in the air.

Her horse faltered below her, confused. Then it began picking up speed. Eyeing its saddle, Madeleine pushed against the lance and released her grip. She plummeted downward, hoping to time her trajectory right. Hoping that the laws of physics she had learned from Xenophilus—angles of momentum, vectors and velocity—would save her life.

With a loud *whomp*, she landed heavily on its back. The horse let out a baffled whinny. Its legs nearly gave out, but fear took charge and it dug in harder.

"In the name of—*come back here, you coward!*" shouted King Henry from behind her.

The horse was heading at full tilt toward the palace's stone gate. Four feet thick, it had been opened to let out an ornate, gilded black carriage. Now the gate was rising, and the guards stared at her in dismay. "What the devil are you doin'?" one of them screamed, running into her pathway. "Ye'll get yerself killt!"

The horse was frothing now. It whinnied again, picking up speed. At the last second, the guard leaped out of the way.

Her eyes on the retreating carriage, Madeleine held tight as the horse squeezed through the gap.

●●●●●

"There, Father! That'll be the tree!" Master Winthrop said, pointing through the window of the royal carriage.

"Are ye sure, son?" his father said. "It looks like every other tree in the forest."

"The knothole. It's in the right place. The two branches like the arms of a dancer!" Winthrop barely waited for the carriage to stop before he leaped out.

Luke Cahill grabbed a torch as his son raced to the knothole. Although it was morning, the thick tree cover made the forest dark. Luke had given clear instructions. They were to reach in to that hole together. He could not risk the clumsiness of an eleven-year-old's fingers destroying anything fragile. If the girl had hidden something crucial—his father's full list of ingredients, perhaps . . .

Or was it *their* father's? His and the girl's? All night, in his dreams, he had seen Madeleine's face—her features transforming into Olivia's and then Gideon's. Her mannerisms were so like Jane's, her voice nearly identical to Katherine's. What if she *were* his sister? How could he countenance her death?

"Father, come!" Luke was snapped back into reality by the voice of his son. His only *real* family.

You sentimental fool, he scolded himself, walking toward the tree, *you must not be swayed by a face. The world is full of traps.*

Winthrop waited by the knothole, his hands clasped together, dancing from foot to foot with excitement. "May I look? May I at least look?"

Luke lit the torch. Ignoring the boy's request, Luke walked past him and peered into the knothole. He adjusted the torch, but even at full light, all he could see was a gray lump at the bottom.

He reached in carefully, hoping it was not a dead animal—or, worse, a live one with sharp teeth.

His fingers closed around a limp, shapeless mass. He grasped as much as he could, lifted the thing out, and spread it onto the forest floor.

Gray pants. A gray shirt. Gray socks stuffed into rough, black leather shoes. A gray woolen face mask. Disgusted,

Luke reached back in but extracted nothing more than wood chips, acorns, and a handful of agitated ants.

"Those were her clothes!" Master Winthrop said. "She was wearing these when she robbed the marketplace!"

Luke's mind reviewed the layout of the market. The fruits, vegetables, meats on the south end—and the cobblers, tinkers, and clothing merchants to the north. "She had stolen a change of clothes . . ." he said. "She needed something presentable for the interview. She changed her outfit here."

Winthrop giggled. "She took off all her clothes outdoors?"

"She was hiding only *clothing*!" Luke said, kicking the garments in frustration.

"Can you let her go, then, Father?" Winthrop said. "She really is lovely. And . . . well, have you thought of taking a new wife? The king likes to do that, you know—"

Enough. Luke glared at the boy, and he shrank back.

Behind him sounded the clattering of hooves, swift-moving and strong. Luke glanced up to see trees moving near a blind corner behind his son.

"Winthrop!" he shouted, yanking his son off the road with one hand.

As they both dove away, a team of colossal horses thundered by. Luke sheltered his son with his body as soil and branches rained over them. He heard his own driver shouting in shock, followed by the shriek of horses and the crack of splitting wood.

It was over in an instant, but not before Luke had a chance to see the receding carriage.

Its color was black and deep purple, with a gilded V painted on its side like a bolt of lightning. Through the oval of the rear window, Luke spotted a shock of black hair with a streak of silver.

Vesper.

Luke felt his blood rise. Nineteen years had only sharpened his rage at the murderer of his father.

"What was that?" Master Winthrop asked.

Luke's own carriage lay in splinters at the other side of the road, the horses bolting into the woods and the driver wandering dazedly.

"It is the man who made me what I am," Luke said between gritted teeth. He grabbed his son by the scruff of the neck. "Follow me!"

●●●●●

Damien Vesper hated the countryside. Too much fresh air led to high spirits. And high spirits made people into idiots.

The smell of fear calmed his soul. And right now it wafted toward him full strength from the seat opposite his.

"I—believe that was Lord Cahill's carriage," said the valet Hargrove.

Vesper had never seen a man sweat so much. It was

downright unseemly in a grown man. "The *late* Lord Cahill, I would imagine," Vesper replied. "Alas, drivers these days . . . so reckless! I will have to speak to mine."

He smiled agreeably, but the man remained stone-faced. How dreary. Years ago, the help could carry on real conversations — not just sit like lumps, expecting to be entertained!

Just as well, he thought. *This one has outlived his usefulness.*

"You did good work, Hargrove," he said, holding out his hand. "Took the training quickly, used uncanny powers of observation. I am impressed at how you were able to recognize the ring. I will have it now."

"Of course, Your Lordship, but you promised five hundred pounds in advance." Hargrove's sweat was dripping from his nose, which struck Vesper as inconsiderate. Especially from one who expected rewards.

"I said I would *advance* you five hundred pounds," Vesper replied. "Which sum would be payable upon receipt of the ring!"

"I — I have seen an inscription on it," Hargrove blurted out. "And for another few pounds, I can tell you what I think it means — "

"Inscription?" This was getting interesting. In recent years, Vesper had heard of a secret ring. But he had never connected this ring to Gideon Cahill.

It had taken him nearly two decades to track down Olivia. He'd intended to force out the secrets to Gideon's

PETER LERANGIS

serum but failed again. How delightful to discover there was a daughter. When he'd seen her hiding at the funeral, everything just . . . fit.

She was fiddling with a ring. And his memory flashed back to her father and the last conversation he'd had with Olivia. He thought she was a grieving widow then, and not another conniving Cahill.

Now he knew better.

"What inscription did you see?" he pressed. Following Madeleine, bribing the servant — all of that had been child's play. He had no room for his lackey's stubborn attitude.

"If I am to reveal the ring," Hargrove said, swallowing hard, "I must have your word that —"

Vesper heard a soft zing. Hargrove fell silent, his mouth agape. He clutched the side of his neck and fell to the ground.

"Do not play with me, man," Vesper said. But as he knelt over Hargrove, he heard another zing, and another. He flattened himself to the floor and slapped Hargrove in the face, hard.

That was when he noticed the small dart stuck in the servant's neck.

Bandits. Vesper grabbed a firearm, a long arquebus, from under the carriage seat. "Move!" he cried to the driver. "Faster!"

His coachman whipped the horses. They took off through the woods, the carriage bouncing wildly.

Vesper climbed out of the rear and nearly vaulted toward the driver.

A set of hands grabbed him from behind.

Vesper twisted his body around. He dug his elbow into the attacker's neck and raised his arquebus high.

With a grunt, he brought the butt down hard. The attacker tried to duck away, but the gun caught his shoulder. Vesper could see him now—slender, dressed in black, including a mask that covered most of the face.

Lifting his foot, he gave the thief a kick.

With a cry, the black-garbed figure fell over the side. His gloved fingers gripped the railing, and he struggled to keep his feet off the swift-moving ground.

Vesper caught his breath. With a smile, he pinched the gloved hand's pinkie and lifted it off the railing. "This little piggy went to market . . ."

He flicked the next finger off, and the attacker sank lower.

Now the bandit's feet were scraping across the roots and ruts. He let out an odd, high-pitched scream—almost a woman's voice.

The carriage bounced violently again. Vesper flew backward and felt the small of his back hit the joint of the carriage frame. He clenched his teeth with the pain.

The fun was over.

He lifted the arquebus and pointed it at the intruder's head, which was fast sinking over the edge of the carriage. Releasing the shuttlecock, he placed his finger on the trigger.

A deafening crack split the air. Vesper felt the recoil of the firearm, the smell of gunpowder. But his shot had gone off course. He rose into the air and then smacked back down sharply. The carriage was careening side to side, its wheels tilting inward at the top, wobbling.

"The axle!" the driver shouted. "She's splitting, milord!"

On the edge of the carriage, Vesper caught a glimpse of the intruder's fingers, struggling to regain a hold. This bandit had dismaying agility and strength.

Forget him, he can't hold on forever, Vesper scolded himself. He caught a glimpse of Hargrove. He had to get the ring from that fool and then jump off before the carriage smashed to splinters. He dove into the cabin, reaching into the pockets of the unconscious valet. *Where did he hide it?*

There. His money belt. Vesper ripped it open and pulled out the golden prize.

With a wild, triumphant smile, he sat up and held it high. There was enough light to see a string of tiny symbols.

Holding tight to the ring, he scrambled toward the front of the carriage. He couldn't keep his footing. The wheels were slanting, the carriage bottom scraping the ground. In a moment the axle would split in two. The driver's seat was already empty. *So much for loyalty.*

As Vesper prepared to jump, he saw a movement

beneath him. He tried to look down, but his feet lifted off the surface. He was flying.

His vision filled with the trunk of a thick oak tree, racing closer. He drew his arms in for protection. And he screamed.

The last thing he saw before impact was a great black shadow.

●●●●●

"Help!" Master Winthrop cried out. It had begun to rain. He felt scared. Why had Father run ahead of him? It was dark and cold.

There. Just ahead. He could see Father in his cloak, crouching on the ground.

At that moment he was glad for the rain. Maybe it would disguise his crying. Father never liked it when he cried.

As he drew closer, he slowed. The carriage — the one that had nearly killed them — was scattered across the forest in pieces. It looked as if Father had taken the whole thing apart himself.

"Father?" he said.

Master Winthrop crept closer, his heart beating like a bunny rabbit's. His father remained silent, his back to Winthrop. In the distance, two men had been tied to an old oak tree. He recognized old Hargrove, and the second man was dressed in a livery suit. There appeared to have been a third captive, but he had managed to escape, the ropes in a heap beside the tree.

"Are they . . . alive?" Winthrop said, placing his hand on his father's shoulder.

But Luke Cahill's eyes remained fixed on the ground in front of them. It had been smoothed. Etched deeply into the soil, in precise letters, was a message that made Winthrop's blood run cold:

1942. Most of the world was at war. In every corner of the globe, people were fighting and dying for one cause or another.

And what was Grace Cahill doing at this critical moment in her planet's history?

Changing diapers.

Not diapers—nappies, she corrected herself, deftly fastening a large safety pin at each of the child's small hips. Here in Europe they used the British term.

Baby Fiske burped loudly and tried to wiggle out of her grasp. Grace held on with a firm hand. Parts of the lawn at their family's villa in Monte Carlo were so steeply sloped that a wayward toddler might roll all the way down the bluff and drop into the sparkling waters of the Mediterranean.

She called him Kamikaze sometimes, after those crazy pilots from the *other* war—the one in the Pacific. Fiske always seemed to be looking for some great peril to hurl himself into. The little stinker was walking, so it had become nearly impossible to keep him out of trouble. He was a year old now. Grace could scarcely believe it had been that long since . . .

She had gotten good at fighting back tears. Her stomach, though, was harder to control. She recognized the feeling from her flying lessons — the sensation of hitting an air pocket and dropping five hundred feet in a matter of seconds. She experienced it on solid ground every time she thought of her mother.

"You have a healthy baby son," the doctor had informed James Cahill, "but your wife . . ." He said more, but their father's raw, tortured breathing filled in the blanks for Grace and her older sister, Beatrice. Father shed not a single tear over the death of his wife, but he was never the same. His reaction seemed more appropriate to a record-setting marathon run than an expression of grief — hyperventilation and drenching sweats.

Not that the Cahill daughters had much opportunity to develop an instinct for their father's emotions. The time he had spent in Monte Carlo since the funeral could be measured in days, possibly hours. James Cahill was so devastated by the loss of his wife that he wouldn't even look at his newborn son. He had turned to travel, as if trying to outrun his grief. The family had not heard from him in months, save for the occasional postcard from exotic locales — Rio de Janeiro, Baffin Island, Ulaanbaatar.

Baby Fiske yanked a croquet hoop out of the ground, and Grace barely managed to wrest it from his hands before he could plunge the ends into his eyes. How was it possible to love a child so deeply when he was the author of all the suffering in your life? His birth had cost Grace her mother. And it was costing Grace her father, too. The picture of James Cahill walking out the door was permanently imprinted on her retinas. He'd claimed to be leaving on business "for a few days." But his vast pile of luggage—enough to require a second taxi to follow him to the airfield—revealed the lie. She could still feel Father's arms around her as he said good-bye. He'd seemed like a drowning man holding on to a life preserver. Beatrice had noticed the same thing.

Then he was gone—without so much as a sideways glance at the bassinet that held his infant son.

Fiske reached for the croquet hoop, howling in frustration as Grace held it just beyond his grasp. She scooped him up in her arms and carried him, kicking and screaming, to the main house. Someday, she told herself, her brother would be a contributing member of society. Just as someday this war would be over, and someday Father would come home. That was what her life had become: too many *somedays*; not enough *nows*.

"How can you take care of that little beast?" came a sharp voice behind her.

Grace wheeled. She hadn't seen Beatrice standing by the doorway.

"Someone has to," Grace replied. "Giselle won't. Leave it to Father to abandon us with a useless governess."

"How dare you speak that way of Father?" Beatrice snapped. "Did you expect him to go on as if nothing happened? He lost his wife."

"And we lost our mother," Grace put in.

Beatrice pointed an accusing finger at her brother. "Thanks to *him*!"

Grace hugged Fiske, shielding him from the acid in their sister's words. Could Beatrice blame a baby for what had happened to their mother? Or was it that the older girl was so miserable herself that she had to make everybody else miserable as well? The sisters had never been close. Yet since Edith Cahill's death, the chasm between them had grown even wider.

Didn't Beatrice see that Grace was suffering, too? That Grace would have given anything to reverse the events of the past year—to bring Mother back, to undo the pain that was tearing the family apart and had already driven Father away? The one thing she wouldn't change was Fiske. How could Beatrice not love this bundle of giggles and mischief? Motherless—and basically fatherless, too. James Cahill hadn't bothered to name his only son. He had left that to Beatrice. *Fiske.* It was Beatrice's secret revenge on her brother, condemning him to a childhood of fistfights and taunting.

Grace ran her fingers through the little boy's fine blond hair. This hellion was the only good thing that had happened to them in a long time.

Fiske repaid the sentiment with a kick to her stomach that sent her reeling. His feet were already pumping like pistons by the time she dropped him. Teetering unsteadily, he ran out the door to his croquet hoop and who knew what other dangers.

With an apologetic glance at her sister, Grace followed.

•••

Sleep did not come easily to Grace these days. It had started with the bombing across the border in France. They were safe — Monaco was neutral so far, and even France had quieted under German occupation. But slumber continued to elude her.

Clad in her nightdress, she gazed out the window at the dark Mediterranean. From the nursery in the next room came the buzz saw of Fiske's snoring. Another quality Beatrice found so endearing. Enlarged adenoids.

Grace frowned. There was a second sound — a low rumble — distinct from her brother's.

An outboard motor? She remembered the times when pleasure craft dotted the sea, day and night. Now it was too dangerous. France was under German control, and Italy was only ten miles away.

Yet when she squinted into the gloom she could make out a small boat a few hundred yards offshore, almost directly opposite their villa. A weak flicker was coming from the wheelhouse.

Are their lights not working? Grace wondered. *And now they're lost in the dark?*

During wartime, wandering off course could be a fatal mistake.

And then she recognized the pattern of short and

long flashes. Her eyes widened. This was not the product of any guttering lamp. It was something she'd learned from her father several summers ago.

Morse code.

It took a moment to decipher the opening salvo of dots and dashes.

JC

James Cahill! The message was for her father!

She scrambled for pencil and paper, converting the dots and dashes into language as she expertly transcribed the message. She'd been only seven or eight when he'd taught her, yet she didn't miss a single letter. Beatrice received high praise and high marks from their private tutor, but Grace was the sister whose quick and nimble mind was capable of occasional brilliance. This wasn't boasting; it was simply the truth.

VS KNOW ABOUT BULLS EYE . . . GO TO WHITE
HOUSE AM . . . FIND GSP . . .

A pause. Was that all of it?

The Morse code resumed:

TORCH IS MORE THAN IT SEEMS . . .

She peered out, waiting breathlessly for the rest. More flashes came, and her wrist jumped to action. But no — it was merely the message repeating.

At last, the motor swelled and the small craft began to move off.

Come back! she wanted to scream. *What does it all mean?*

A final burst of code:

PROTECT THE RING AT ALL COSTS

"What ring?" she said aloud. But the boat was gone.

She had no idea what any of it meant, but one thing was certain: The people on that boat believed they were communicating with James Cahill.

Grace had not lived to the ripe old age of thirteen without realizing that there was something special about Father's family. Her parents had told her and Beatrice how Cahills had shaped human history for centuries. Some of the most famous people of all time were cousins—Shakespeare, Mozart, Abraham Lincoln, and even Babe Ruth. Secret words had passed between her parents in whispers—*Lucian, Janus, Tomas, Ekaterina,* and one that seemed especially mysterious, *Madrigal.* There was also a number that kept coming up—39. It had been Father's football number at Harvard, but Grace suspected it meant much, much more.

Grace didn't know the specifics of Cahill business—just that James and Edith Cahill had been up to their necks in it. But now she suspected that when Mother died, James had abandoned his Cahill responsibilities along with his children. The people on that boat were trying to communicate with an agent who had dropped out. Another vital role was going unfulfilled.

She stared at the cryptic words on the pad. The

message made as much sense to her as Fiske's childish burbling. *VS*—somebody's initials? No, then it would be *VS KNOWS*. This was *VS KNOW*. So the Vs had to be a group of people. But who?

BULLS EYE—a direct hit. In a war, that could mean almost anything. *GO TO WHITE HOUSE*. Surely not the one where the president lived?

AM—as in morning? Or that could be initials, too. Also *GSP*. Were these people or things? More confusing still, *TORCH* and *RING*—two random items.

She opened her bedroom door and stepped out into the hall. Beatrice would know what to do. She was two years older, and Beatrice was the one their parents had been grooming for a major role in the Cahill family. Grace had only been included when it turned out that her sister had no stomach for flying lessons.

Beatrice always had a fuller understanding of the sudden trips their parents used to take on urgent Cahill matters. Maybe she could decipher the strange communication.

"Bea?" She peeked into her sister's room. "Are you asleep?"

"I *was*," came the reply. No one expressed annoyance more thoroughly than Beatrice Cahill. And she had plenty of practice at it. Everything annoyed her.

"I have to show you something." Grace told her sister of the boat that had come, flashed its message, and disappeared just as abruptly. "Here—I'm turning on the light."

Blinking in discomfort, Beatrice sat up in bed and examined the paper Grace proffered. "It's gibberish."

"Gibberish doesn't come in Morse code," Grace insisted. "It was meant for Father."

"Anybody with a message for Father should know that he hasn't lived here for more than a year," Beatrice retorted.

"Not if it's a Cahill thing," Grace argued. "The family is scattered around the world. Father might have been keeping in touch with them some other way. You understand more about Cahill business than I do."

"I understand enough about Cahill business to stay well out of it," Beatrice said caustically. "There's nothing about that lot that interests me."

"Maybe this is about the war! What if Father and his contacts could help put a stop to it?" Nothing would take precedence over that. Millions had died already, and the conflict only seemed to be spreading.

"Whatever it is you *think* you know about Cahills, let me set you straight. Our family has wasted centuries playing foolish games, stabbing each other in the back and reading all sorts of meaning into meaningless things. If one more coded message shows up for Father, I think I'll scream."

Grace stiffened like a pointer. "There were others?"

Her sister shrugged derisively. "I don't waste my time trying to decipher every moonbeam."

"But, Beatrice," Grace pleaded, "you're the one Mother and Father chose to share the secrets of our family with. Don't you want that?"

"What I want," Beatrice said firmly, "is to be a regular, normal person. The Cahill world isn't normal. I intend to ignore the whole thing. And if you know what's good for you"—she cast her sister a sharp look—"you'll follow my example. Now, go to sleep!"

Grace looked into her sister's eyes. There was another emotion there, concealed by Beatrice's perpetually sour face.

Fear.

She couldn't decipher the message any more than Grace could. But one thing Beatrice *did* understand was that high stakes meant high risks. She wanted no part of the Cahill world because it scared her to death.

Grace withdrew, more disappointed than angry. As usual, there was no talking to Beatrice, who was an immovable mountain when she made up her mind about something.

She looked around at the sumptuously furnished home. Their villa in Monte Carlo was spacious and luxurious, with vast banks of windows that, in daylight, provided breathtaking views of both the mountains and the sea. It had cost millions, and it was only one of five similar residences James Cahill owned around the globe. The wealth alone spoke of their family's power, but money was only part of the story. The huge house was filled with artworks and artifacts Mother and Father had collected on their extended travels. These hailed from all continents—from every remote corner of the map. Perhaps Beatrice could ignore all this proof of the Cahills' special role in human history, but not Grace. The world was in chaos. Father had taken himself out of the picture, and his elder daughter had chosen to do likewise.

The mantle must fall to Grace.

I have to do this myself.

Her eyes traveled to the paper and her resolve mingled with unease. Willingness to do something wasn't the same as knowing what needed to be done.

She set her jaw. Her mother's death; her father's disappearance — these were things beyond her control. Her immediate family was unraveling, but *this* part of it — her parents' involvement with the Cahill clan — could still be saved.

If she could decipher the cryptic message.

The question remained: How?

●●●●●

Madame Fourchette was in a towering rage. "What shall I say to your father when you grow up ignorant, you silly girl?" the tutor shrilled. "Why can you not be more like your sister?"

"Impossible," Grace said blandly. "Beatrice is one of a kind."

"Beatrice has done her assignment, and you have written not a single word! I will have the reason why!"

There was a reason, not that Grace was going to

share it with Madame. For the past week, her every waking moment—and even her troubled dreams—had been devoted to trying to make head or tail of the message from the mystery boat. She had scoured the villa's extensive library and even begged entry into the larger one at the Prince's Palace, home of the ruling Grimaldis. As far as she could figure, there was absolutely nothing to connect people called Vs, a bull's-eye, the White House, morning, a torch, and a ring. As for GSP, that was the most baffling part of all. She could not seriously believe that her father was being directed to find a German shorthaired pointer, the Georgia State Patrol, or a green spotted puffer fish.

"As I suspected, you have nothing to say for yourself," Madame Fourchette told her sternly. "Since you cannot seem to write your essay, you will instead write five hundred times 'I must complete the schoolwork assigned to me.' At once, *s'il vous plaît*."

Grace felt a headache beginning to gather behind her eyes. The thought of all that mindless scribbling when there was important work to be done made her both angry and depressed.

As she descended the spiral staircase, she heard the sound of breaking glass coming from the entrance hall. Fiske, no doubt, destroying yet another priceless piece of art. Where was Giselle? The answer came from the radio in the parlor—music from the BBC in London. The governess enjoyed English programming much more than she enjoyed trying to control a one-year-old wrecking crew.

Grace sat down at the table and scribbled out three quick lines. Great. Only 497 more to go. She was about to begin line 4 when the music stopped in mid song.

"We interrupt this program for a news bulletin. The Allied invasion of North Africa has begun. Yesterday morning British and American troops landed at Algiers, Oran, and Casablanca in a three-pronged attack known as Operation Torch. The Casablanca force, under the command of American general George S. Patton . . ."

The report went on, but Grace had heard enough.

George S. Patton — GSP!

Operation *Torch*. And Casablanca — that was Spanish for *white house*! The Morse message hadn't been about the White House in Washington at all! Father was being sent to Casablanca to seek out General Patton, who was commanding Operation Torch!

It was bizarre, and yet from a Cahill point of view, it made perfect sense. If Ben Franklin, Napoleon, and the Russian royal family could be Cahills, why not George Patton? And surely the general would be able to decode the rest of the message — the Vs, the bull's-eye, and the ring.

Her heart pounded with the exhilaration of discovery, but the feeling soon turned to despair. Father was completely out of reach. By the time she could pass this information on to him, Operation Torch would be in the history books. Could she get in touch with General Patton? How? Through the American embassy maybe?

Oh, sure. The US military will put an invasion on hold and call up a general on the say-so of a thirteen-year-old girl.

The dilemma nearly tore her in two. Now that it was clear that the Morse code message was connected to Operation Torch, who knew how vital Father's mission might be? If the Cahills were as powerful as Grace had heard, it could turn the tide of the entire war! And then millions would be spared the kind of suffering Grace's family had known.

The world needed Father, and he was nowhere to be found.

She stopped short, frowning. No, that wasn't quite true. The world needed a Cahill — and Father was not the only one. Grace was a Cahill, too.

What am I thinking? I'm not in charge of saving the planet! I'm thirteen years old! I'm not even allowed out of the house without permission!

Casablanca was hundreds of miles away, across the Mediterranean. It was difficult to reach under the best of circumstances. Right now the place was under attack. She'd never get there. And even if she did, she'd probably be killed.

The feeling that came over her at that moment caused her to put down her pen and stand up behind the mahogany table, shoulders squared. It was the deep sense that, against all logic, she *belonged* in this fight. It was her place to be there, no matter what the consequences.

She had no way of knowing it, but members of her family had been answering that call for nearly 450 years.

● ● ●

Monaco to Casablanca.

Overland, it was a journey of more than a thousand miles, across defended borders, through countries in conflict. And then she'd still need to traverse the Strait of Gibraltar to get to Africa.

Travel by ship would be more direct, but the Mediterranean was dangerous during wartime. More to the point, boats were slow. By the time she reached Casablanca, General Patton might be gone. And the opportunity — whatever it was — would be lost.

An airplane, then. Maybe, just maybe, a lone plane could carry her to North Africa without attracting the attention of all the warring powers.

Grace's brow darkened. If the warring powers weren't going to be thrilled about this, Beatrice was going to be even less thrilled — not to mention Giselle and Madame Fourchette. And somewhere, when the news of Grace's disappearance reached Father, he was going to blow a gasket — if James Cahill even remembered the family he'd left stranded in Monte Carlo.

Well, there was simply nothing for it. Cahills had been changing the world for centuries. If there was ever a world that needed changing, it was this one.

Grace's suitcase lay open on the bed, empty but for one item—her passport. The future she was heading into was so completely unknowable that she couldn't think of a single necessary thing to pack. Fresh clothing? Where would she find a place to change? A toothbrush? Was there running water on a battlefield? In the end, she pocketed the passport and stuffed the suitcase back in her closet. The only thing that seemed fairly certain was that she would be running for her life. Luggage would only slow her down.

What was really required here was money. Cash opened doors and greased palms and hired planes. There was plenty of it in Father's safe, but only he had the combination. This was not for lack of trying. Many times Grace had scoured the house for a hint of what the numbers might be. Not that she intended to steal from her father. She'd always had a sense that access to the safe might come in handy one day. And, she reflected ruefully, she'd been right.

Stealthily, she crept into her father's study. She could hear Fiske in the kitchen, demanding a cookie in English, and Giselle arguing with him in French. Grace smiled in spite of herself. As if a baby would understand or even care. She had little doubt that her brother would win his cookie. He rarely took no for an answer. She felt a sharp pang at the sound of his shrill voice. She was about to abandon him—just as Father had abandoned them. She had every intention of coming back, but the mission she had planned for herself was fraught with so many risks that she couldn't wrap her mind around them all. And those were just the hazards she could foresee.

She was not like Beatrice, the eternal doom-crier. But she had to admit to herself the very real possibility that this journey might turn out to be a one-way trip.

If I die, who will be here to love Fiske?

She shook herself and returned to business. The safe.

She already knew the first number to try—39. Whatever it meant, it was central to the legacy of the Cahill family. She was convinced that her father would use Cahill references in his combination. Mozart's birthday, perhaps—James was a huge admirer of their composer cousin. January 27.

Holding her breath, she twisted the dial. 39-1-27.

Locked.

Abraham Lincoln, then. February 12—39-2-12.

Locked.

She tried Howard Carter—May 9; Emperor Puyi of China—February 7; and the Grand Duchess Anastasia—June 18. By now, beads of perspiration stood out on her brow. It was sinking in that there were hundreds of famous relatives—and dozens of numbers associated with each of them—dating back to the fire that destroyed Gideon Cahill's lab in 1507.

Wait a minute! 1507! 15-07!

She turned the knob—39-15-7. Fingers trembling, she reached for the handle.

GORDON KORMAN

Her face fell. Locked.

She'd known from the start that she might fail in this adventure.

But not before I get out of Monte Carlo! Not before I even get out of the house!

All at once, her downcast features rearranged themselves into a quizzical expression. She tried the numbers again, this time in a different order.

15-7-39.

There was a metallic click, and she swung the heavy safe door open.

Wow.

It was more money than she'd expected—a lot more. Stacks of bills bound with rubber bands—French francs, British pounds, Italian lire, German marks, and American dollars. There was even a canvas bag of gold coins. She took a leather briefcase with her father's initials and stuffed in as much as would fit. In normal times, it would have been enough to take her to the North Pole and back. But this was war. Everything was different now.

"I'm going out for some air," she called to whoever might be listening. The lump in her throat as the door shut behind her was larger than she'd anticipated. This wasn't home, really. But it was the last place Mother had lived, and every memory was precious.

She got on her bicycle and started off down the shore road. It would have been comical if the situation hadn't been so grave—pedaling off to war with a fortune balanced in the wire basket of your bike. She had an insane desire to ring the bell.

Their villa was not far from the airfield because nothing was far from anything else in a country that was smaller than one square mile. Monaco was a perfect jewel, with its cathedral and medieval palace perched on a rocky promontory on the coast. She had always considered it the loveliest place on earth. Now it would always be the place where Mother had died. Its beauty no longer existed for Grace. Its spectacular winding hills merely made cycling a chore.

She pedaled up to the airfield and left her bike leaning against a wall. The building was tiny, with a doctor's office–style waiting room and a single counter. "Excuse me, monsieur," she told the clerk, placing her open passport on the desk. "I wish to arrange transportation."

The man looked down his long nose at her. "Where is your father, mademoiselle?"

Grace was not intimidated. "*I* am the one traveling, not my father. I need to get to Casablanca, in North Africa."

The man's shock turned to laughter. "Casablanca? Even as we speak, mademoiselle, Casablanca is under attack! It is no place for a little girl!"

"Luckily, I'm not a little girl," Grace said coldly.

"Even so! There are no flights to Casablanca! No one is flying there except for the purpose of dropping bombs!"

"I realize that," Grace conceded. "I'm here to charter a plane."

"Presuming you are able to find a pilot reckless enough to go," the clerk blustered, "he would demand a king's ransom to risk his aircraft and his very life in this way."

In answer, Grace set the briefcase on the desk and flipped it open.

The man's jaw dropped so low that she half expected him to knock his teeth loose against the counter. "I will consult with the pilots!" he exclaimed in a strangled voice, and disappeared through a swinging door into a back room.

Grace snapped the case shut, suddenly self-conscious. She might not be a "little girl," but she was a ripe target for robbery.

The clerk returned after barely a minute. "It is as I told you, mademoiselle. No one is willing to take you to Casablanca."

Grace tapped the case. "There's gold in here as well."

He favored her with a full body shrug that was very French. "A dead man would have no opportunity to spend it. I am sorry, but this disappointment is probably prolonging your life."

She withdrew, feet dragging, the bag heavier than ever. Briefly, she considered using the money to buy a plane and trying to fly herself, but quickly abandoned the idea. She did not yet have her pilot's license, and her navigation skills were as likely to take her to Sweden as North Africa.

A feeling of helplessness took hold in her gut. If

no pilot would fly her, what could she do? She couldn't pogo-stick across the Mediterranean!

She was climbing back on her bike when a low, heavily accented voice startled her.

"Why you want to go there?"

* * * * *

The dark, unshaven man who stood before Grace was built like a stone toad—short, with no neck and a torso so hulking it didn't seem likely that he'd fit in a cockpit. Part of the problem might have been his voluminous ratty fur coat that looked like it had come from a woolly mammoth.

"Are you a pilot?" she asked.

"Is war in Casablanca," he persisted. "Why you want to go?"

"That's my business," she told him sharply.

"My business is staying alive," he told her evenly. "If I have brains, I don't go there. If I have money, I don't go there."

"And do you have those things?" Grace asked, trying to hide her eagerness.

"It will cost much," he warned.

"I'll pay you ten thousand American dollars."

The man's bushy eyebrows jumped, but his voice remained impassive. "Twenty—in advance."

"All right. Twenty—when we get there."

"How I know you have this money?" he demanded.

Grace shrugged. "How do I know you have a plane?"

He grunted. "Come back—midnight. Wear black. You bring money. I bring plane. If anybody asks, you never spoke to Drago."

Grace had the audacity to fly into a war zone in search of an invading general, but she lacked the courage to return to the villa. Once reunited with baby Fiske—and even disagreeable Beatrice—she was afraid she might never leave again.

At a store by the palace, she bought black slacks, a black blouse, black boots, and a black leather coat. The clothing was expensive, designed for hobnobbing with high society, not for a desperate night flight. Still, money was the one thing she had plenty of—as opposed to wisdom, or experience, or even a clear plan of what she was going to do once she got to Casablanca. If this was her first test as a Cahill, she was pretty sure she was failing miserably.

She toyed with the idea of renting a locker for her old clothes but ended up throwing them in the trash. This was no game. Operation Torch was an actual shooting battle. There was a very real chance that she might not survive this adventure. But even if she did somehow come through it all, she had a sense that she'd never be the same again. The Grace Cahill who wore frilly flower-print dresses and adored romantic novels and movies was gone forever.

As night fell, her thoughts returned to her family. Were they anxious about her back at the villa?

Probably. She could only hope that Beatrice would hold off calling the police until Grace was airborne.

11:55. She pushed her bicycle into a drainage ditch, hefted the briefcase, and walked out onto the deserted airfield. All was dark except for a dim light coming from one low hangar. She made for it, heart pounding in her ears.

As she drew closer, the biplane came into focus — hulking, dilapidated, patched with tape and fabric. Crudely painted on the fuselage was a name: *OLGA*.

A gasp of dismay escaped Grace.

Drago loomed out of the shadows. "You were expecting brand-new B-29?"

"No — it's just — can this thing make it to Casablanca?"

"No," Drago replied.

"*No?!*"

"The fuel will take us as far as airstrip I know near Valencia, Spain. From there *Olga* can reach Casablanca."

Grace regarded the aircraft. "It doesn't look like *Olga* can get off the ground."

Drago was insulted. "My *Olga* won the first Zurich-Mombasa air race. She dropped supplies to partisans in Seville. She landed in cyclone in Istanbul when it was still called Constantinople."

She sighed. "I guess we'd better get going, then." She reached into the briefcase and pulled out a fat bundle of bills. "Ten thousand. And another ten when we get there."

He snatched up the money and stuffed it into the depths of his voluminous coat. "I am not greedy. Ten thousand is plenty if it means I don't have to go to Casablanca and get killed. Farewell, foolish girl."

Grace was outraged. "We had a deal!"

"Here is advice to pass to your grandchildren some-day: Trust no one."

In a rage, Grace brought the heel of one of her new boots down on his soft shoe. He howled in pain and reached for her, but she was already vaulting into the cockpit of his plane, pulling down the canopy as she dropped to the seat. In a flash, she had the engine running and was beginning to taxi out of the hangar.

He tried to block her way until the whirling propeller drove him back. He watched in astonishment as his beloved *Olga* rolled out onto the tarmac and headed for the runway. In a horrified instant, he realized that the plane was not stopping.

Drago sprinted headlong across the airfield and hurled himself onto the lower wing of the biplane. Undeterred, Grace began to taxi in a serpentine motion in an effort to shake him off. Hanging on for dear life, he crawled between the struts to the fuselage, reached up, and managed to flip open the canopy. *"Stop!"*

In answer, Grace opened the throttle, sped down the runway, and pulled back on the yoke. With a mighty roar, the biplane left the ground.

Watching the airfield fall away from him lent strength to Drago's panic. He hoisted himself up and over, and tumbled into the passenger seat. "All right," he wheezed. "I will take you to Casablanca."

"Why should I believe you?" she shouted over the roar of the engine.

He was wide-eyed. "Because you have proven yourself worthy of my fear!"

When the aircraft crossed the border into occupied France, Drago was at the controls and Grace was in the passenger seat, hugging the briefcase to her chest.

Her journey to Casablanca had begun.

••••

Their flight path followed the coastline, not that Grace could tell. Occupied France was under strict blackout orders, so there were no lights beyond the occasional wisp of illumination sneaking out from behind dark curtains.

Drago navigated by starlight and the dim glow cast by a crescent moon. Occasionally, he consulted a torn and ratty map that lay open on his lap.

Grace squinted out the window into the gloom. "How do you see where you're going? I can't even make out where the water meets the land."

"Don't have to see," the pilot grunted. "*Olga* knows the way."

"Funny name for an aircraft," Grace commented. "Is it after your wife?"

"My gun."

Grace stared at him. "You named your plane after a *gun*?"

"It was very good gun."

She scanned his shaggy, inscrutable features, trying to determine if he was serious. One thing was certain: He could not be trusted. He had already tried to double-cross her once and wouldn't hesitate to do it again.

For the present, though, the pilot seemed content to be piloting, and the biplane jounced above the coastline, plodding southwest. Grace did not remember sleeping, but she awoke with a start, instantly aware that something was different. There was no longer unbroken darkness below them. Lights shone from farmhouses and the occasional village.

"We're off course!" she cried. "You're taking me to the wrong place!"

He shook his head. "We have crossed over Spanish border. No war here."

"Sorry." She was chastened but relieved. Fascist Spain sympathized with Germany but was technically neutral. Where there was no fear of bombing, there were no blackout restrictions.

"You have father?" Drago asked her suddenly.

"Why should you need to know?" Grace demanded.

He shrugged. "I am father. My daughter, I hope, will never go on purpose to a place of battle."

"Well, my father is out of the picture," Grace said bitterly, "so I can't know his opinion on this or anything else."

"He is dead?"

Grace shook her head. "Just—gone. He left us." As much as she resented James Cahill for that, she would have given anything to see his face right then. Mother, too—her fair features, pale skin, and auburn hair. The gentle way she spoke your name, even when she was angry. The kindness that radiated from her . . .

No, don't think about that! Father might come back, but Mother never will. . . .

"I, too, did this thing. Left my family." Drago's gravelly voice betrayed no emotion. "I hope one day my daughter will understand."

"What's to understand about your own father deserting you?"

"Some things you must do," he informed her. "To make money. To survive. If this was not true, I would not be taking you to Casablanca."

In the reflected light of the instrument panel, Grace peered at her pilot. Every wrinkle and pockmark, she imagined, had probably been etched by some cruel happenstance or experience.

Life is hard for everybody, not just the Cahills. . . .

Drago's voice interrupted her reverie. "In one hour we stop to refuel. If there is fuel."

"If?" she echoed in alarm. "You mean there might not be?"

"Wartime," he said grimly. "Even neutral countries have rationing."

"But what if we can't take off again?"

He shrugged. "General Franco's men are not known

for their trust. I will be arrested as spy. Your youth might save you. Maybe."

Valencia appeared in the distance, glittering against the dark coastline. There was an otherworldly quality to being suspended in midair, in the cold and gloom of *Olga*'s cabin, passing over Europe's storied cities. Despite the tension of the moment, Grace felt strangely free. It was almost as if the crippling fact of her mother's death, her father's disappearance, even the responsibility of caring for Fiske couldn't find her up here.

Drago veered inland, skirting the city to avoid attracting unwanted attention. Half an hour later, a double row of lights appeared amid the inky fields.

"Is that it?" Grace asked anxiously. For the past ten minutes, she had been watching the dropping fuel gauge. Pretty soon they were going to have to land, whether it was in the right place or not.

Drago nodded. "I told you. *Olga* knows the way."

Whether credit was due to *Olga*'s knowledge or Drago's skill, they were soon down on a concrete runway, taxiing toward a stack of fuel drums.

Drago pulled the biplane to a halt and killed the motor. When the propeller sputtered to a stop, Grace realized how much *Olga*'s vibration had become a part of her. It had been four hours since they'd left Monaco. Her guts were shaken; her lungs were full of gas fumes. And here they were—nowhere.

Drago popped the canopy and heaved his bulk out of the cockpit. "I will refuel." He pointed to a small shack. "In there you will find toilet."

Grace glared at him. "If you think I'm going to give you the chance to fly away and strand me, you're crazy."

He shrugged. "It is long way to Casablanca."

"I'm fine, thank you very much."

"As you wish." He jumped to the tarmac.

A few minutes later, she heard the clanging of the metal drums and the gurgling of liquid filling the biplane's tank.

She tried to stretch out her stiff legs, but in the cramped cockpit, there simply wasn't room. She forced herself to ignore the discomfort. This was, after all, the easy part. They were about to fly into a war in search of an invading general. She should appreciate this calm while it lasted.

And then something cold and hard prodded her arm. She looked down at the barrel of a machine gun.

● ● ● ● ●

A black-clad Spanish officer stood on the bottom rung of the boarding ladder. "Your papers, *señorita!*"

Frightened, Grace fumbled in her coat pocket and came up with her passport.

The Spaniard's eyebrows rose. "American. You will come with me."

"Why?" she demanded in outrage, summoning an imperious dignity she did not feel. "You have no right to arrest me. I've done nothing wrong."

"Your country is at war, and therefore so are you. You are to be detained for questioning by the government of Generalissimo Francisco Franco. You will step out of the aircraft."

"I — can't." How could she ever explain it to a man with a machine gun — that if she left the plane, Drago might fly off and abandon her?

Speaking of Drago, where was he? The refueling sound had ceased. Was the tank full and the pilot in hiding, waiting for the officer to drag her away?

The gun nudged her again. "Out of the plane, *señorita. Ahora!*"

Grabbing the briefcase, she climbed down and submitted to being marched across the tarmac toward a small hut marked POLICÍA.

Grace's mind was awhirl. Could she bribe the man? What if he thought she was some kind of spy? If she got sent to a prison camp, no one would ever find out what had become of her! Even if they interrogated her and let her go, she'd be marooned in the middle of Spain.

Either way, she would never make it to Casablanca.

There was a loud thud, followed by the clatter of the machine gun falling to the tarmac. A split second later, the Spanish officer hit the ground beside his weapon.

Grace wheeled. There stood her pilot, brandishing a large wrench.

He took her hand and began to rush her back to the plane. "Hurry! He may be light sleeper!"

Weak with relief, Grace allowed herself to be stuffed

back into the cockpit. Minutes later, they were in the air once again, crossing the Spanish mainland.

Grace gaped at her strange, shaggy pilot. "You could have left me! You could have flown away!"

Drago indicated the briefcase, which was once again in her lap. "Where my money goes, I follow."

"You already have ten thousand dollars," Grace reminded him. "In Monaco you said you weren't greedy."

He refused to look at her. "Do I resemble smart man to you?"

"You resemble a *wonderful* man!" she breathed.

"Bah!" he scoffed. "Where we journey is no place for sentiment."

"I'll pay you more money," she promised.

He nodded. "I deserve it."

•••

An hour later, they were out over the Atlantic Ocean, giving Gibraltar a wide berth to avoid alerting the British Royal Air Force installation there.

They had left Europe behind. Next stop: Africa.

Operation Torch came into view before Casablanca did. The first rays of dawn revealed a towering plume of smoke obscuring the African coastline.

"Look—" Drago pointed. "There is your war."

Grace gulped. "I was hoping it was just—bad weather."

But now she could see hundreds of ships of all sizes—a mammoth naval battle. From this distance, they looked like Dinky Toys. Grace had to remind herself that every faint flash of orange represented an explosion of enormous destructive power. American fighter planes strafed and dive-bombed the defenders, unchallenged by any Vichy French air force. In the sea she could make out the vector-straight track of a submarine-launched torpedo. Amphibious landing craft spilled their invaders onto the beach. Thousands of troops, tiny as ants, swarmed over the sand, exchanging lethal fire with the French soldiers dug in there. The scene was all the more bizarre because Grace couldn't hear anything over the noise of *Olga*'s engine. That left a ghastly pantomime of mechanical monsters and soundless death.

"How are we going to get past all that?" Grace shrilled.

"You ask me this *now*?" he demanded bitterly.

"I thought . . ." Her voice trailed off. The truth was she *hadn't* thought. She had brought them to this carnival of destruction with no clear plan.

Drago had an idea. "We go around it, of course. We do not want to tangle with one of your American — how do you say — hotshot pilots." He veered back out to sea, flying parallel to the coast, avoiding the thick of the battle. The strategy was to come ashore well south of the city. They would approach Casablanca's airfield from the east, away from the fighting.

They were close enough that Grace could make out the minarets of Casablanca through the smoke. She wondered which of the American fleet was the heavy cruiser USS *Augusta*, Patton's ship.

"There is problem," Drago said suddenly.

It all seemed like a problem to Grace—bombs dropping, cannons firing, bullets flying, shells bursting. Even from afar, it was the utmost in chaos and insanity.

"What's wrong?"

"Our fuel is low," Drago replied.

"How low?"

His expression was grim. "We must land now."

"What—in the middle of all that?"

"Now!"

He turned *Olga* toward the city and began to descend, veering closer to the teeth of the clash. "Airfield is just beyond town. I can make it!"

"But you're heading straight into the war!" she cried. "It's not safe!"

"Safer than crashing into the ocean!"

Her eyes were riveted to the canopy, watching as they edged nearer to the smoke of the battle. Fifty yards . . . twenty . . . ten . . .

Stay out of it . . . she prayed, twisting her shoulders as if her body language could alter the plane's inevitable course.

And then the conflict surrounded them like a fatal fog. The aircraft began to vibrate as Drago cut speed.

Grace could feel the concussion of exploding artillery shells. The fighting was no longer silent. Bursts of flak bloomed all around them.

With a sharp crack, a stray fragment of antiaircraft fire tore through the fuselage.

Drago turned to Grace. "Now you will land *Olga* yourself."

"Me? Why?"

"Because I will very shortly be dead."

And then she saw the blood pooling on the moth-eaten fur of his coat where the shrapnel had pierced his chest.

●●●●●

Horror surged through her. "You're hit!"

"We must change seats"—his voice was strained—"while I can still move."

"We have to get you to a doctor!" she shrilled.

"Do it! There is very little time." He leaned forward, literally stuffing her into the seat behind him. At last, he collapsed into the passenger chair.

Grace took hold of the yoke and throttle, fighting to steady her trembling hands. "You have to tell me what to do!"

The sight of him terrified her. The whole front of his coat was now saturated with blood. His face was chalk-white, his lips blue.

"You will do it," he promised in a thready voice.

"How can you know that?"

He stared at her as if memorizing her face. "I lied about Olga. She is not my gun. She is my daughter."

Grace struggled to control the shuddering craft.

"I have not seen her since she was small child,"

Drago whispered hoarsely. "But it is my hope" — he coughed — "that she is growing up to be like you."

Grace tore her eyes from the horizon for just a second. It was long enough for her to realize that the pilot was gone from her. Drago was dead.

Not even at her mother's funeral had Grace wept with such intensity. She had dragged him here on her mad mission, and it had cost him his life. It was her fault as surely as if she had shot him herself.

But there was no time for regret. Below her was the beach — American troops shooting up at defenders on higher ground. *Olga* was now low enough to be in the thick of the fight. Rifle fire whined all around her like deadly mosquitoes. A stray bullet tore through the fuselage inches from her elbow and exited through the canopy.

I will not die here! Grace gritted her teeth, wrestling with the controls as the biplane crossed over the shore. *I will live on and have children and grandchildren who will never have to go through terrors like this just because they're Cahills!*

She eased up on the throttle, gentling *Olga* lower and lower until the highest buildings of the city were passing mere feet beneath the landing wheels.

Where was the airfield?

A sputter from the engine told her that she did not have the time to find it. Drago had been right. The fuel tank was running dry. She was soon going to be on the ground one way or another.

Beyond Casablanca, the vast desert loomed. All

right—if she couldn't locate the airfield, she was going to have to set down on one of the roads that led out of the city. She could see ribbons of pavement criss-crossing the sand.

Her flight instructor had been James Cahill, which meant that she had not had a lesson in more than a year. It was a bad time to be rusty, but there was no point in lamenting that now.

Speed equals altitude had been Father's motto. Less throttle meant more descent. The biplane swooped low over windswept dunes. The road was directly in front of *Olga*'s nose. Grace went for it, all focus.

With a cough, the engine burned its last drop of gasoline. The propeller stopped, and *Olga* was falling. The crash was jarring. One tire blew, and the struts on the other collapsed. Sparks flew as metal parts scraped against the pavement at high speed. The plane spun off the road into the sand.

Grace's world turned upside down, and she reached out a hand to brace herself against the control panel.

Impact. Blinding pain.

Darkness.

• • •

It began as a general ache all over her body. But as Grace awoke, it localized. Her arm was in agony. She struggled out of her coat and examined the damage. Swollen, misshapen, and black and blue to the elbow. She must have broken her wrist in the crash.

The pain was awful, but not nearly as awful as the sight of Drago's lifeless body tossed like a rag doll in the seat beside her.

She looked up and instantly regretted it. The sun was overpowering—and very high in the sky. She must have been unconscious for hours.

Using her good hand and her teeth, she ripped out the lining of her overpriced coat and fashioned a sling for her left arm. It still hurt like mad, but at least it was supported. She popped open the canopy, swung a leg over the side, and dropped to the ground.

The plane was a total loss. The collision with the sand had torn one of the wings, and the tail was broken off. Smoke billowed from a spot behind the propeller.

"Drago—" she whimpered. How could she abandon him to the desert? Yet she could do nothing for her pilot now. A dead man had no use for company. To the money in the briefcase she gave not a single thought. Its sole purpose had been to buy her way to Casablanca. And here she was. In the general vicinity, anyway.

In the process of landing she had overshot the city by several miles. It was going to be a long hike, and she had best get started.

She began to trudge along the road in the direction of the distant spires and minarets.

It grew hotter. She took back everything she'd ever said about Boston winters. A snowdrift would have been heavenly for both cooling and drinking purposes. Her thirst was beginning to occupy all her thoughts.

Time passed—at least a couple of hours. The sun was well past its zenith in the cloudless sky. She could feel the skin on the back of her neck roasting. Dressing in black had been a good idea for sneaking through the night at the Monaco airfield. Yet here in the desert, it was practically suicide, absorbing the solar heat as it did.

Her broken wrist throbbed with the jolt of every step. Still she soldiered on, driven by a mixture of courage and stubbornness. Perhaps she had not fully understood what it meant to be a Cahill when she embarked on this adventure. But each sizzling foot of sizzling sand brought that truth home to her: There was no pain. There was no heat. There was no exhaustion. There was only the task at hand.

The sun pounded down on her unprotected head. All around her, the baking desert shimmered. She could barely make out Casablanca, although she had to be a lot closer to it now. And the smoke plume from the battle—it had *moved*! It was off to her right. Low and trailing across the dunes like a long snake all the way to the horizon.

Oh, no! Was she starting to lose her mind? Everyone knew about desert mirages.

She heard the growl of an engine—*many* engines. An army jeep appeared in the midst of the dust cloud. And another, followed by a truck. An entire convoy of military vehicles veering toward her on an intersecting road.

This was no cloud! It was an army!

The Vichy French? How would Casablanca's defenders treat a US citizen — even a young girl — after the terrible bloodshed in the harbor and on the beach?

And then she spotted the star insignia on the side of a half-track.

Americans! The battle was over. These were the conquerors — Operation Torch's Western Task Force — rolling triumphantly into the city.

An instant before, Grace was convinced that she had not a single ounce of energy left. She was wrong. The sight of the military column lent wings to her feet. She sprinted right into the middle of all that roaring machinery, waved her good arm, and yelled, *"Stop!"*

Out of the heat haze of dust and sand lumbered a Sherman tank, its gun turret pointed directly at her. The caterpillar treads clattered to a halt. The hatch opened, and a helmeted head emerged.

"Are you crazy? Get out of the way!"

"I'm an American!" Grace shouted through dry, cracked lips. "I have to see General Patton!"

The soldier laughed harshly. "I'll check his calendar. *Get out of the way!*"

Grace drew herself up to her full height, which barely cleared the top of the tank tracks. "Tell the general that Grace Cahill has an urgent message for him!"

"Hold it!" came a shout.

A jeep swerved around the tank and pulled up beside Grace. A young captain jumped to the road. "Did you say your name is *Cahill*?"

"Grace Cahill. I've come a long way to see the general."

The man looked her up and down. "I'll say."

He loaded her into the jeep, wheeled off the pavement, and began to plow through the sand, passing a procession of soldiers, tanks, and equipment that easily stretched back thirty miles. The BBC broadcast had estimated that the Western Task Force numbered 34,000 troops. Grace was not surprised. The jeep's spinning tires must have kicked dust and dirt over at least that many.

After what seemed like an endless ride, they pulled back onto the road, blocking the path of a very large staff car.

The driver stuck his head out the open window. "What's the holdup?"

The captain snapped a rigid salute. "Grace Cahill to see the general!"

"Cahill?" echoed a gruff voice.

The door opened and two shiny boots hit the tarmac.

Grace stared dumbly. The officer who stood before her radiated confidence and command, from his ramrod-straight posture to his armor-piercing gaze. Although he had just finished masterminding and directing a three-day battle, his uniform looked clean and pressed. On his helmet gleamed two stars.

It was General George S. "Blood and Guts" Patton.

Bodies littered Casablanca's beachfront, and spilled fuel burned in the waters of the harbor.

The battle was over.

The Vichy French defenders had surrendered, so the city was peaceful. The tranquillity belied the brutal reality of a bloody invasion that had cost nearly two thousand lives, more than a quarter of them American.

Grace rode into town in the staff car next to Patton himself. Although she was champing at the bit to tell him about the Morse code message, she kept quiet. The commander was surrounded by aides and bodyguards. There was no way to be sure who — if anyone — could be trusted to hear the top secret communication that had been meant for James Cahill. Her only option was to wait until she was alone with the general.

When they reached the building that had been selected for Patton's headquarters, Grace was attended to by his personal physician. Her broken wrist was set in a plaster cast, and she was given food, water, and a room to rest in. She slept for the first time in more than thirty hours and awoke to find fresh new clothes ready for her. On the dresser sat her briefcase. A good sign — it meant the contents of the plane had been recovered, including the body of the pilot. She popped open the lid. There was the money, every dollar, franc, and mark. The soldiers of Operation Torch were men of honor. It brought her a measure of relief. She could trust the US Army to give Drago a proper burial.

The general came in to see her at 1900. Finally, Grace had what she was looking for — a private audience with General George S. Patton. She explained who her father was and told the general of the mysterious boat that had flashed its Morse code at the villa in Monte Carlo.

"GSP — that's you, right? You're one of the Cahills, like Abraham Lincoln and Mozart. *White house* is Casablanca, and *torch* is the invasion."

He nodded, amazed. "And you tracked me down in the middle of my own war! You're just a kid!"

She bristled. "I'm thirteen."

"Well, the fact that you made it here is better identification than a passport and a blood test," he said with a laugh. "You're a Cahill, all right."

"But what does the message mean?" she asked. "Who are the Vs?"

"There's a group called the Vespers," he explained. "They go back as far as the Cahills. We've been rivals for centuries."

Grace nodded thoughtfully. "They must be the people we have to protect the ring from. But what ring? And what's this bull's-eye the Vespers know about?"

The general held up his hand. "Grace, listen to me. I don't want you to worry about it anymore. You brought me the message. No one could ask you to do anything beyond that. What you've accomplished is a miracle. Leave the rest to me. I'm going to get you, your sister, and your baby brother home to Boston. And it may take some doing, but I'll find your dad as well. You've got George Patton's word on that."

Never before had Grace met anyone so totally in control, so impressive. From the powerful set of his jaw to the forest of ribbons, medals, and decorations on his chest, he was the ultimate American hero.

She didn't mean to cry, yet once the tears began, she couldn't hold them back—the sheer relief of having so much burden lifted from her shoulders. She wept for Drago, for her poor parents, for the very world itself suffering under this awful war. How strange that now—when she was finally safe—the emotion should pour out.

The general's legendary efficiency was evident in his plan for her. Tomorrow morning, she would be on a six o'clock plane to Lisbon; from there, on to London, where she would be joined by her family. Beatrice was going to have a lot to say about her disappearing act. But nothing could spoil the prospect of seeing Fiske again. . . .

Yet there was something vaguely *unsatisfying* about the whole business. She had made an improbable journey at an impossible time; a man was dead, his aircraft destroyed. And now she was expected to walk away and forget any of it had ever happened.

That's good news! she admonished herself. *You have your life; you're being reunited with your family; you've placed the message in the hands of the most competent, confidence-inspiring military man on the face of the earth. How could things possibly go any better?*

Well, for starters, she reflected, the general could have been more specific about his strategy. He'd promised to handle it; what he hadn't mentioned was how. Not that she didn't have faith in him. But Cahill business wasn't Patton's top priority in Casablanca. He was the commander of a conquered city. Hundreds, maybe even thousands, of urgent matters would require his attention. What if Grace's message just slipped his mind?

Sure enough, the general was gone all evening, assessing casualties and equipment losses after the invasion. That left Grace to stew in her doubts, wandering around headquarters under the watchful eyes of officers and sentries.

The place was really a large mansion. Patton's aide had told her that a wealthy Casablanca family had graciously offered their home to the US Army. She couldn't help wondering how much choice the "gracious" owners had in the matter. Then again—she thought of Father's many residences around the globe—the rich usually had someplace else to go. So many had sacrificed during this terrible war. Her sympathies were probably wasted on a single displaced millionaire.

Besides the men in uniform, the only other sign that the mansion had become an army installation was the large city map spread out on a vast dining table. A number of locations were marked with colored tacks—headquarters itself, the officers' billets, and troop deployments. There were pins all over town, except for a central district not far from the beach, filled with very narrow, winding streets. It was surrounded by a solid line on which someone had scribbled the word *WALL*.

She squinted. The area had a name, printed on the paper in paler ink:

ANCIENNE MEDINA

She recalled from Madame Fourchette's French lessons that this meant the old Arab quarter, or casbah.

Her heart began to pound. Ancienne Medina — AM!

So it doesn't mean morning. *When the message said* White House AM, *it was a reference to Casablanca's old casbah!*

She had to inform the general!

"I'm sorry, Miss Grace," said Patton's aide. "He's tied up with military matters. I don't know when he'll be available again."

She returned to her room, growing more restless by the second. The Morse code pointed to the Ancienne Medina, but Patton didn't know that. And by the time she had a chance to tell him, it might be too late. There could be a Vesper in town at this very moment. And the Vespers knew about the bull's-eye, which was a lot more than Grace could say for herself. How could she be certain of what *bull's-eye* might mean in the middle of a shooting war fought with weapon scopes, rifle sights, crosshairs, and targeting systems?

She was positive that the answer lay somewhere in the casbah.

But the general had said her part was over. . . .

Well, that was then; this is now.

She could not stand idly by, giving their rivals a chance to find the bull's-eye first while Patton was distracted by military matters. She had to help. She owed it to the general; she owed it to her family; and she especially owed it to Drago, who had lost his life getting her here. Somehow, she had to make that meaningful.

She'd never be able to explain this to the sentries stationed about the mansion. Luckily, Grace was an expert at sneaking in and out of places — training from her role as the younger sister of tattletale Beatrice.

She opened the shutters and eased herself over the windowsill, contemplating the eight-foot drop. Hanging on with her good hand, she lowered herself as far as she could and then jumped the remaining distance to the ground. Keeping to the shrubbery, she sneaked across the property and vaulted a low wall.

For a place that had just been seized by foreign invaders, Casablanca seemed very much business-as-usual. The streets were bustling with veiled women, turbaned and white-robed men, and visitors of a wide variety of nationalities. With war raging on the continent to the north, this part of Africa had been the first stop for many civilians trying to escape the conflict. People went about their business, heads down, never making eye contact. It was perfect for Grace's purposes — nobody looked at her. But it contributed to an overall sense that something secret was going on.

She had memorized the route between headquarters and the Ancienne Medina, although she questioned her navigation skills more than once along the way. The roads did not appear to be laid out on any kind of grid. They twisted and turned, and the exotic arabesque architecture, with its elaborate designs, made it impossible to fix on any landmarks.

She was relieved when at last she arrived at the stone wall, weathered by centuries of sand and dust storms, surrounding the Ancienne Medina.

She had made it—but where to go from here?

Inside the casbah's gates, the neighborhoods were older and more crowded. Some of the alleyways were so narrow that the upper floors of the Moorish buildings almost met above the road, creating a tunnel effect. There were no cars here, just swarms of pedestrians and a few bicycles and carts. Tiny stalls and shops sold everything from live chickens to expensive jewelry. Saloons, restaurants, and cafés lined both sides of the street as far as the eye could see.

1001 NIGHTS proclaimed a pink neon sign. Open shutters revealed tiny tables and dim flickering candles that made it nearly impossible to see the food. This, thought Grace with a shudder, might be a plus. Two men were playing darts in the back room, and money was changing hands.

Grace stared. A dartboard.

Bull's-eye—the center circle of a dartboard!

Flattening herself against the crumbling stucco, she waited until the two gamblers finished their match and stumbled off to the bar. Then she slipped into 1001 Nights and made her way to the dartboard in the rear.

She peered at the bull's-eye. There were just a few holes, some of which looked like they had been made by knives and not darts. She reached behind the board. Nothing but wall — rough plaster, no secret compartment.

Okay, wrong dartboard. But there had to be plenty of others in the Ancienne Medina. Too many. And the only way to find the right one was a door-to-door search.

A voice too close to her ear said, "Would the young lady care to challenge an expert?"

Grace was back out on the street before she could formulate a refusal. She wasn't sure why she was so scared. After all, hadn't she just crash-landed a plane in the desert? Yet it took all her resolve to get her into Scheherazade next door. Belly-dancer music spilled out from a broken window. Oh, joy.

The next three hours saw her in and out of some of the sleaziest nightspots in all of North Africa. She examined dartboards of various shapes, sizes, and degrees of disrepair, stained with food, grease, and even, she suspected, blood. The bull's-eyes yielded nothing.

The search was making her nauseous. It was getting late. A thirteen-year-old American girl in some of these places attracted attention. It was only a matter of time before she became a curiosity or, worse, a target. Maybe General Patton was right. Her job was done. It was crazy for her to try to take this any further in such a strange and dangerous environment. Especially since she had no way of knowing which of Casablanca's hundreds of taverns she sought.

Her eyes fell on the very last neon sign on the winding street:

Her mind raced back to the Morse code message: *Torch is more than it seems.*

She had always interpreted it as a reference to Operation Torch. But it could just as easily have meant: Torch is more than the name of the invasion; it marks the location of the bull's-eye.

The Torch Singer Café seemed busier than the others. That might have been because it was long and narrow, more like a hallway than a tavern. It had a tiny stage for a lone performer, and—she checked very carefully—no dartboard.

Disappointment. She'd been so sure.

And then she noticed the back door, partially hidden behind a trolley piled high with dishes. A fly-specked window overlooked an isolated alley. The dark courtyard was dominated by a large bronze sculpture of some kind of animal.

She strained for night sight, taking in the stout, powerful body and curved horns.

A bull.

Bull's eye — not the kind on a dartboard but the actual eye of a bull!

She pushed the trolley out of the way and heaved at the sticking door, which came open in a shower of ancient paint chips. Examining the statue up close, she spotted it instantly. One eye was a rounded piece of green glass. The other socket was empty.

"They beat us to it," said a deep voice from the shadows.

Grace wheeled. She didn't recognize him at first in tan slacks and a pale blue shirt — civilian clothes. But there, out of uniform, stood George S. Patton.

"General — what are you doing here?"

Patton smiled grimly. "Same as you, my dear. You're a true Cahill, Grace, sneaking out under the noses of my entire staff. You'll be a great asset, even though you're not much for doing what you're told."

She could not be distracted. "What happened to the bull's eye? Who beat us to it?"

The general raised his eyebrows. "The Vespers, of course. They always seem to be a step ahead of us."

Grace was skeptical. "We Cahills are the most powerful family in human history."

"We are, we are," Patton said quickly. "But the Vespers have one advantage over us. They're *not* a family. They recruit only the best and the brightest—ruthless geniuses of diabolical brilliance. While we Cahills are held back by infighting among the family branches, the Vespers can be completely and perfectly united behind their goal:"—his steely eyes gleamed—"world domination. Yes, they're our rivals, but there is much to admire about them."

"No," whispered Grace, devastated. She had come so far, risked so much—and at that, she was luckier than poor Drago. How could Patton just give up? Cahills didn't do that!

"But this Vesper agent"—she persisted—"he could still be in Casablanca. He might have only beaten us by five minutes! We have to find him! You've got a whole army at your command. We could catch him, and search him—it's a ring he took, right?"

"I admire your spirit, cousin," Patton told her. "Don't worry about a thing. When I leave Casablanca, I guarantee that I'll have the ring. Now, come along. My jeep is waiting."

As he turned to take her arm, Grace caught a glimpse of his breast pocket. It bulged, concealing something just about the size of the bull's empty eye socket. With a manufactured sigh, she slumped against him, making sure to brush the mystery object beneath the fabric of his shirt. Hard, probably metal, with a rounded band.

Holding in the shock and rage she felt, she followed him out of the alley and got into the back of his jeep. The general had no way of knowing that this slip of a girl had discovered his secret.

Yes, the Vespers had beaten the Cahills to the ring. And, yes, Patton would not leave Casablanca without it.

How was that possible?

The Vesper was Patton himself.

* * * * *

Grace's first challenge: bury her anger. Nothing must be allowed to interfere with her thinking.

In the next suite of rooms, she knew, Patton was asleep for the night, enjoying the double triumph of a successful invasion and a Vesper victory. The importance of the ring had to be colossal. Operation Torch had three landing points. Patton must have persuaded the entire US Army to choose Casablanca as one of them just to get himself to the bull's eye. Ruthless geniuses, he had called the Vespers. It was all too true. And Old Blood and Guts was the most ruthless of the lot.

But this wasn't over yet.

Once again, she left her room via the window, this time shuffling along the narrow ledge that circled the house. Moving her bare feet an inch at a time, she edged toward the balcony that was outside the main bedchamber—the general's suite. It was a warm night and the French doors were open. She slipped inside, walking lightly. To her right, she could hear Patton's deep breathing. To her left was the dressing room, with the general's uniforms hanging in military precision.

She found the pale blue shirt he'd been wearing last night and reached eagerly for the pocket.

Empty.

Don't panic. It stands to reason he'd keep it close. . . .

She glided into the bedchamber, the rich rug absorbing any sound she might have made. She scrutinized the nightstand. There was a pitcher of water and a half-full glass. Holding her breath, she slid open the drawer. A gold watch, nothing more.

Leaning over the bed, she tried to see his hands. Oh, what would she do if he was wearing it? But his fingers were bare.

Her eyes fell on a wooden valet, which held his clothing for the morning—a dress uniform with a chest full of decorations. He certainly wanted everyone to see the evidence of his heroic career. Those medals were more important to him than anything—except maybe the ring.

Grace's eyes narrowed, and she moved in for a closer look. What better place to hide a piece of jewelry than amid all that brass and gold?

She stared. There it was, between a French Croix de Guerre and his Purple Heart. It was fastened to a red-white-and-blue ribbon and pinned to the jacket—just one award among dozens.

The ring.

She removed it, taking another medal from the end and filling in the empty space. Pocketing her prize, she quickly and silently flitted back out the window and returned to her room via the ledge. At last, she examined the focus of so much attention from both Cahills and Vespers.

It was about the size of a man's class ring, yellow gold. Around the band was a peculiar design of embossed ridges and tiny slots. It wasn't much to look at, so it must have had some hidden function or meaning.

Never mind what it is. The important thing is you have it, and Patton doesn't. . . .

Now the trick would be to sneak it out of Casablanca before the general realized it was missing.

She stepped out into the hall, where she was immediately challenged by the sentry at Patton's door.

"Sorry, miss. I'm not supposed to let you leave."

"Oh, I'm not leaving," Grace replied airily. "I'm just going down to the dispensary for an aspirin." She hefted her cast. "My arm is very sore."

The soldier nodded sympathetically and waved her on.

She breezed down the stairs and into the room where the doctor had set her arm. From an instrument tray, she found a scalpel and began to dig a trench in the hard plaster on the underside of her cast. She worked furiously. If this took too long, the sentry would come looking for her. When the hole was big enough, she jammed the ring inside and wet a length of plaster bandage. She wrapped it over the ring, shaping and smoothing it so it would blend in with the rest of her cast. Tidying as best she could, she returned just as the sentry was beginning to descend the stairs in search of her.

"Find your aspirin, miss?"

"Yes, thanks. I had a hard time getting the cap off with just one hand."

The hall clock said 3:30. Two and a half hours to her flight.

Sleep tight, General. Sweet dreams.

●●●●●

The first thing General Patton noticed the next morning was that his Bronze Star was in the wrong place.

Unacceptable. Even the lowliest buck private in the Western Task Force knew better than to mess with a commander's medals.

He bellowed for his aide, but before the first syllable had passed his lips, he knew. The ring was gone.

It was the girl, of course. She was really something. Still, she wasn't going to get away with it.

His aide burst into the room. "Yes, General!"

"Call the airfield! Grace Cahill's plane is not to take off from Casablanca!"

The man blanched. "It's already gone, sir. Miss Grace was anxious to get moving, so we took her to the airfield early. She was the only passenger and—"

"I want that plane turned around and the little witch brought to me in chains!" the general howled.

The aide winced. "She has already landed in Lisbon—under Portuguese jurisdiction. I'm sorry, General. There's nothing we can do."

"Get out!" Patton rasped, and the officer ran for his life.

Beaten—and by a thirteen-year-old girl!

Those Cahills! They had been a thorn in the side of the Vesper organization for more than four centuries.

He was about to go up against the entire German army, but he feared it less than that cursed family!

They had regained control of Gideon Cahill's ring. And now they had a new champion—a girl with the courage and guile to outflank George S. Patton.

●●●

At the airfield outside London, Grace hugged baby Fiske and tried to smile at Beatrice. Her sister wasn't buying any of it. "What do you have to say for yourself, Grace? Where have you been? What happened to your arm?"

Grace gazed at the spot on her cast where the new plaster covered the precious ring. "This? It hurt for a while, but now it feels fine."

Beatrice was beside herself. "That's not what I asked! How *dare* you run off on us in the middle of a war? Who do you think you are?"

Grace took a deep breath. The past two days had been the most difficult of her life, and she knew that there were many others ahead. She felt the weight of her wonderful and terrible family settling on her slim shoulders, and the answer to her sister's angry question suddenly became obvious.

"I know exactly who I am. I'm Grace Cahill."

Windchill stuck at zero.

Check.

Piles of dirty snow on sidewalks.

Check.

Math test tomorrow.

Check.

Complete lack of preparation for test.

Check.

Social Studies Boredom Level: Ten.

(Sigh). Check.

Dan Cahill's Existence: Situation Normal!

Dan tried to focus. Ms. Zapata's mouth was moving, but the words were a blur of sound. Occasionally, something poked through, like *Etruscans*. Once, *bloody battle* got his attention until he lapsed back into boredom again.

He'd been trapped in social studies for about a hundred hours. Okay, forty-two minutes and thirteen seconds. It was the last class of the day, and it was so fascinating he could hardly stay asleep. He

JUDE WATSON

stared out the window at the slate-gray February sky and tried not to yawn.

Back in September, in the middle of the Clue hunt, if he'd thought about being in social studies class again? It would have seemed like heaven on a stick compared to getting chased, double-crossed, and almost killed by his relatives. When he and Amy had touched down at Logan Airport after their adventure, they'd both cheered. They couldn't wait to get back to their lives. They couldn't wait to be just like this: bored out of their minds.

They'd just made one major miscalculation. They'd forgotten how boring being bored could be. Why hadn't Dan remembered Ms. Zapata's nickname? Everyone called her Ms. Zzzzz because she put her students to sleep.

The funny thing was, Dan had actually *experienced* what Ms. Zapata was now droning about. He'd been to Egypt. He'd felt the heat and tasted the dust. He'd felt a thrill slipping down the dark Nile in a boat past the Valley of the Kings.

Ms. Zapata made it sound like she was reading instructions on how to install a dishwasher.

Just then a word floated out through the buzz saw of Zapata-speak: *Nefertari.* Dan tuned back in.

". . . the most beautiful tomb in Egypt," Ms. Zapata was saying. "You probably know the queen because there's a famous bust of her."

A photo flashed on-screen.

Dan raised his hand. "That's Nefertiti," he said. "Different queen."

Ms. Zapata frowned. She looked at her notes. "You could be right, Dan. Uh . . . let's move on."

Another slide flashed on-screen. "Now, this is the inner chamber of the tomb, where she was laid to rest."

Dan's hand rose again. Ms. Zapata closed her eyes.

"Actually? That's the side chamber."

"Really." Ms. Zapata's lips pressed together. "And how do you know this, Dan?"

"Because . . ." Dan hesitated. *Because I was there. Because I was locked inside the tomb with an ex-KGB spy, so I got to know it pretty well.*

"Especially since the tomb is closed for conservation," Ms. Zapata said.

Yeah. But we had this connection to an Egyptologist? Except he turned out to be a thief and a liar, so we captured him. I came this close to smashing him with a lamp. . . .

Everyone was looking at him. Dan didn't know what to say, and *that* never used to happen. He'd been back at school for four months, and the story for their five-week disappearance was that he and Amy had to take care of family matters after their grandmother's funeral. Nobody was supposed to know that they'd been chasing Clues all over the world. Nobody was supposed to know that he'd been locked in a tomb. Or been shot at, buried alive, and almost blown up.

"I guess I saw it somewhere," he mumbled.

Ms. Zapata tried not to look pleased. "Let's try and remember not to make claims that aren't true, shall we?" She let the moment hang there as everyone twisted in their seats to look at Dan. He knew they were waiting for him to be Dan The Man, to snap back a comment that would be funny but not disrespectful enough to get him in huge trouble.

"Sure," he said.

Triumphantly, Ms. Zapata turned back to her notes. His classmates swiveled around again, disappointed that Dan hadn't caused Ms. Zapata to turn that awesome magenta color she did when she was aggravated.

Four months ago, he and Amy had thought it would be easy just to go back to their old lives. But it hadn't been easy. Dan knew that he'd changed. He didn't know how, exactly—he just knew he was different. It wasn't a kick anymore to contradict his teachers or make the whole class laugh.

Maybe it was the lack of sleep. Sometimes his nightmares scared him so bad he had to sleep with the lights on. He couldn't seem to connect with his old friends. He couldn't seem to care about the cool things he did before, like comic books and video games and the chances of the Red Sox taking the Series next season.

He'd become a loner. Which meant, in the world of middle school, he was tipping on the scale straight down toward Loser.

When the bell rang, he popped up quickly and scurried out the door. He made for the exit and didn't breathe freely until he hit the cold February air.

Amy's school was four blocks away, and they always

met halfway, in front of a coffee bar. After school, if it was a good day, there would be a cinnamon roll left at the coffee bar. There was a loading zone in front so that Fiske or Nellie could park the car temporarily and wait if they had to.

It was a Wednesday, so it would be Fiske today. Nellie, their other guardian, had an afternoon class at Boston University. They usually heard Fiske before they saw him because of all the horns blowing as he cut across traffic. Fiske must have gone to the NASCAR School of Driving. He said that Boston traffic was a challenge and he was its master.

Amy was always worried that he'd get a ticket. That was his sister. If she didn't worry about stuff that didn't matter, he'd have to check her pulse.

When they got back to Boston, he and Amy wanted everything the same, including moving back into their apartment. But now that Fiske and Nellie were their legal guardians, it wasn't too long — barely a couple of weeks — before they all realized it wasn't going to work. The apartment was just too small.

Fiske had the perfect solution. They moved out to Attleboro, to the guest house on their grandmother Grace's property. Fiske devoted himself to the plans for rebuilding Grace's mansion, which a fire had almost completely destroyed. But the guest house was perfect, with a big country kitchen and room enough for all of them. Dan had a bedroom overlooking a field and an oak tree. Amy had a room with a canopy bed. Saladin had a window seat overlooking the garden. It had been easy to settle in.

Especially since they were now massively rich. In addition to the two million they'd received for finding their ancestor Gideon's serum, it turned out that Grace had left the rest of her estate to them in trust. Which basically meant that they were something close to bazillionaires. It was a weird feeling. He and Amy could probably get driven to their old schools in a limousine every day, but they knew they weren't limousine people.

They had no idea how to be rich.

"Snack time," Dan said as he approached his sister. "Fiske isn't even in sight. He's probably going a hundred in a fifty-miles-per-hour zone as we speak."

Amy peered down the street. "He could be here any minute."

"C'mon, Amy, cinnamon rolls are calling us." Dan put a hand near his ear. "Do you hear? 'Amy? Dan?'" he squeaked. "'Come and get my sugary, sticky goodness!'"

Just then he noticed that Amy had that look, as though she wanted the street to buckle and split so she could fall right in. Dan saw the cool crowd from her school hanging at a table in the front. So *that* was why she didn't want to go in. Evan Tolliver was at the head of the table. Dan sighed. Evan, the human computer, was Amy's dream crush. Whenever Evan was near, she got her stutter back.

"Oh, excuse me, I didn't notice Luke Skywalker," Dan said. "Or is it Darth Vader?"

"Shhh," Amy said. Her cheeks were red. "He's coming."

"You mean Evan Tolliver himself is about to set his foot on the sidewalk? Did you bring the rose petals?"

"Cut it *out,* dweeb!" Amy said fiercely.

"Hi, Amy," Evan said from behind her.

Amy's color went from summer rose to summer tomato. She shot Dan a look that told him he was in serious trouble.

"Hey, Evan," he said. "I'm Amy's little brother, Dweeb. Great to meet you, man."

Amy turned so that she was blocking Dan from Evan. "H-hi, Evan."

"Wow, I'm glad I saw you. Did you pick a topic for your English paper yet?" Evan asked. "I'm sorta freaked about it."

"Really? I've got a couple of ideas, but . . ."

Dan decided it was a terrific time to hit the mute button that sat ever ready in his head whenever Amy started to talk about school.

Just then he heard a honk and looked over at the line of cars waiting to turn the corner. A motorcycle was weaving through traffic, trying to cut over to the right lane. As Fiske accelerated and made the turn, the motorcycle cut off a delivery truck to follow him. When Fiske pulled over to the curb, the motorcycle pulled in behind him and its rider got off the bike.

The rider was one Big, Scary Harley Dude. He wore leather leggings, a leather jacket, leather boots, and there were probably leather eyes behind his small, round sunglasses.

"Uh, Amy?" Dan said, still looking at Scary Harley Dude, who was slowly taking off his helmet. He had a mass of black curls, but that didn't lessen his epic bad-news vibe. Not one bit.

The Dude took his time strolling toward Fiske. Just to prolong the agony, Dan guessed. Fiske hadn't seen him yet.

He leaned over the passenger seat and waved at Dan. Dan gestured wildly at Scary Harley Dude. The guy had been tailing Fiske, no question. Misunderstanding the gesture, Fiske shook his head and pointed to his watch.

Meanwhile, Amy was still trying to get out a sentence. ". . . was thinking that m-maybe . . ."

"AMY!"

The guy was almost at the open driver's side window. Dan jerked his head toward him and widened his eyes at Amy. They'd been through enough almost-kidnappings, attacks with lethal intent, and encounters with the crazy to have a pretty good instinct about things.

Amy squinted as Scary Harley Dude reached for something at his belt and leaned in toward Fiske. Fiske turned and finally saw him, and they saw fear on his face. . . .

"Noooooooooooo!" Screaming the word, Amy and Dan moved as one.

Time slowed down, which, Dan knew from

experience, often happened when you were in midair. By the time they leaped onto the hood of Fiske's car (oops, dents), and Dan had ripped off a windshield wiper to use as a weapon (probably not the best idea, but hey, he was improvising), Scarey Harley Dude had turned around.

He strode off in his motorcycle boots, moving swiftly to his bike without seeming to hurry. His helmet back on, sunglasses adjusted, he roared off straight into the road, weaving through the thick traffic like smoke.

Amy's face was squashed against the windshield. Dan held the wiper aloft like a club.

And Evan Tolliver stood on the sidewalk, blinking at them.

Dan waved the windshield wiper at him. "Hey, bro. We didn't want to miss our ride."

"Right," Evan said. With a faint, puzzled smile, he turned around and walked back into the coffee bar.

"Are you two all right?" Fiske asked.

In answer, Amy just banged her head against the windshield softly.

"What did he want?" Dan croaked.

"He asked if I was going to be very long," Fiske said. "He wanted a latte. I think you guys freaked him out."

Yeah, I've changed, Dan thought as he handed the windshield wiper to Fiske. *Seeing the potential for disaster in every random encounter? Check.*

Amy had done everything the way she always did. Laid out her source materials. Sharpened her pencils. Cracked open a brand-new pack of index cards. Gave Saladin a pat as he blinked at her and curled up on the edge of her bed. She was ready to start her paper.

If only she could stop thinking about Evan Tolliver's face when she raced across the sidewalk, hurtled over Fiske's fender, and ended up with a face full of windshield.

High school humiliation? She *lived* for it.

Just when she'd managed to have a normal conversation with Evan! He'd actually come outside, just to talk to her! Sure, it was about an assignment, but Amy hadn't thought that Evan even realized she was a carbon life form. He even told her he liked her sweater! He said it matched her eyes. That meant that he'd actually noticed her eyes, didn't it?

Then she'd completely wrecked it by actually listening to her little brother and almost attacking some motorcycle guy who just wanted a cup of coffee.

When Evan went back into the coffee bar, what had he told the others? Would Amy have a new school nickname tomorrow? *Hey, Crash Helmet! Can I borrow your notes, Face Plant?*

Amy closed her eyes and dropped her face in her hands. Her life was over.

Down on the first floor, all was quiet. Usually in the late afternoon Fiske would work on renovating and restoring the Cahill mansion. He had set up a desk in the library, where he had drawings of every room. They'd spent evenings trying to remember every detail of the house that Amy and Dan had loved.

No, the armchair wasn't blue. It was sort of bluish lilacish. Grace said it reminded her of the hydrangeas on Nantucket.

Yes, she hung all her keys on those old brass hooks in the mudroom — she'd bought them in a flea market in Paris.

Fiske took notes and wrote tiny instructions on all the drawings. They wanted to re-create the house exactly as it was when Grace was alive. They would track down antiques, they would replace the stained glass windows in the turret. The deep window seats, the Chinese rug in the study, the scarred wooden table in the kitchen — they would match them as closely as they could. They would bring back as much of Grace as they could. It would cost a fortune, but they had one to spend.

It was funny how the effort to re-create the house brought the three of them together. It was easier to tell stories that were about a favorite chair, or a painting, than to talk about emotions. It was like *Grace* was bringing them together. They were almost a family. But . . . not quite.

Fiske was a hard guy to get to know. It had been weird, in the beginning, to live with a stranger.

Amy knew it had been difficult for him to take on two children. He wasn't used to dealing with things like parent-teacher conferences, slumber parties, buying a Christmas tree. They were lucky they had Nellie and the Gomez family to help. Nellie picked up the slack—she took them shopping if they needed school clothes or notebooks or athletic equipment. She kept track of their schedules and decided on limits of cell phone use and computer controls. Things were working the way they should, if you didn't count that there was a big hole where somebody used to be.

I miss Grace so much, Amy thought. She just wanted to talk to her, tell her that things were basically okay.

Amy raised her head. What was that noise? They usually didn't hear any road noise from the guest house. It was situated down a dirt lane behind the main house, far back from the road. Amy crossed to the window. Shadows were blue smudges on the snow, and the sun was already low in the sky. Nothing was stirring. She must have imagined it.

Then she noticed Nellie's yellow Jeep parked at a crazy angle by the back door, as if Nellie had been in a huge hurry.

But it hadn't *sounded* like the Jeep.

Then she heard voices. *Raised* voices.

Were Nellie and Fiske arguing?

Amy rose from her desk and tiptoed to the head of the stairs in her thick wool socks.

". . . too soon!" Nellie said.

Dan came out of his room and saw her on the landing. He raised his eyebrows.

"They're arguing," she whispered.

"I can't hear anything," he said.

She leaned forward and took the buds out of his ears.

"Are you *sure* they're ready for this?" Nellie's voice was suddenly clear. "We said they needed time. . . ."

That did it. Amy didn't even have to say a word to Dan. They moved together, taking the stairs quickly. There was no way they were going to be left out of this conversation.

They weren't just kids — they were Madrigals. Elite Cahills who had been around the world, faced everything thrown at them. They wouldn't be left out.

"Ready for what?" Amy and Dan both asked at the same time, bursting into the library.

Nellie and Fiske stood near his drawing table by the fireplace. Nellie's fists rested on her hips in the attitude that meant she was ready to fight. Fiske stood tall and pale, dressed in his usual black sweater and black jeans. He turned, startled, when he saw them. For just a flash, Amy saw sadness in his gaze when it rested on them, and her fear began to coil inside her.

"Hey, kiddos," Nellie said softly. "Something's up."

Amy tried to swallow. "What?"

"We wanted to wait as long as we could," Fiske said.

"We wanted you to feel safe, for as long as you could," Nellie added.

Which meant, Amy realized, that they weren't safe. She lifted her chin. "You'd better tell us, then."

"They're Madrigals. It's time they knew."

The voice came from behind them.

Amy turned. They'd been so focused on Nellie and Fiske that they hadn't noticed the guy in the corner. Was it because he was in shadow, or because he was so still?

"Scary Harley Dude!" Dan breathed.

Now that he wasn't wearing his sunglasses, Amy could see his eyes, light gray and piercing.

"Amy and Dan, meet Erasmus," Fiske said.

"You said he just wanted a latte," Amy said with a quick glance at Fiske.

"I just needed to get a message to Fiske," Erasmus said. "He's hard to get hold of. Almost like he doesn't *want* to be contacted."

"I can't imagine what gives you that idea," Fiske said.

"I had to follow him and drop a secure cell phone in his lap."

So that was what he'd been reaching for as they raced toward the car, Amy realized. A cell phone. Not a weapon.

Fiske cleared his throat again. "You might have guessed that Erasmus is a fellow Madrigal."

"Tell them," Erasmus said. He crossed to stand by Nellie. This served to make Fiske seem like he was on a stage, pressured to speak.

Fiske cleared his throat. "Ah . . . where to start?"

"From the beginning," Nellie said. "With Madeleine."

Nervously, Fiske bent to his drawing table and scooped some pencil shavings into his palm. He emptied them into the pocket of his jeans. Fiske did things like that all the time. He was a funny mixture of scatter-brained and incredibly focused.

"Madeleine inherited something from her mother," he said. "When Gideon died, he had passed a ring to Olivia. She guarded it with her life. Madrigals have protected it ever since. Generation after generation."

"Why? Is it so valuable?" Amy asked.

"It's priceless," Fiske said. "We know it was made in the ancient world. But that's not why we protect it. It has a far greater value — we just don't know what it is."

"Grace had the ring," Amy guessed.

"Grace was the last Madrigal to take possession of the ring," Fiske agreed.

"Is it here?" Dan asked.

Fiske shook his head. "It's in a bank vault."

"So . . . what's the problem?" Amy asked.

Because there definitely was a problem.

"Do you remember when, after you got through the gauntlet, we told you about another family, a group who hated the Cahills?" Fiske asked.

"This is not going to be good," Dan muttered.

"They're called the Vespers. They're not blood related, exactly — although at least one of them is descended from Damien Vesper. He was a friend, then a bitter enemy, of Gideon Cahill. We don't know much about the Vespers today — they're a secret orga-nization, and they recruit people. Scientists, captains of industry, military operatives, criminals . . . people who want power and don't care how they get it."

"They want the serum—we know that," Erasmus said. "They also want the ring. They've been after it for centuries, ever since they figured out that the Madrigals were hiding it."

"Do you know who they are?" Amy asked.

Erasmus shook his head. "That's the problem—we've figured out a few possible Vespers, but we don't have hard evidence, and we have no idea who's leading them. We just get reports of activity from time to time that let us know they're still hunting the ring. That activity recently has . . . stepped up. The ring must be moved."

"So where is this ring?" Dan asked.

"In Switzerland," Fiske said. "It's in a safe-deposit box of a numbered account in a Swiss bank. I have the key to it. If something happens to me, the key would go to Amy."

"To me?" Amy asked.

"Grace wanted both you and Dan to be there when I opened the box. She didn't want this day to come so soon," he said gently, looking at Amy. "But she knew you two were strong enough to handle it."

Amy's eyes stung with unshed tears. Every time she heard from Fiske how much they'd meant to Grace, she wanted to break down and blubber like a baby.

"Wait a second," Dan said. "You guys just said that the Vespers are mobilizing. Do you think they're watching us?"

There was a short silence. "It's possible," Erasmus

said. "If so, it would be helpful to flush them out."

"You mean we're bait?" Dan asked. "Sweet!"

"Certainly not," Fiske said. "We would never endanger you and Amy. You've been through enough."

"More than enough," Nellie said firmly.

"We've taken every precaution," Erasmus said. "We made plane reservations from Logan Airport to a tropical resort. Three Madrigals will serve as decoys."

"Including me," Nellie said. "It will be *so* difficult to have to spend five days in Costa Rica, but hey, anything for you guys."

One corner of Erasmus's mouth lifted. "Yes, Nellie, we know how much you hate sunshine and beach towels. The point is—no one will know you're heading to Switzerland. You'll take off from Providence, Rhode Island."

"When?" Dan asked.

"Tonight," Fiske said.

● ● ● ● ●

"It's just like old times," Dan said as they disembarked from the plane in the Zurich airport the next morning. "Three hours of sleep, a lousy breakfast, and I feel like I have a bucket of sand in my eyes."

"That's probably potato chip crumbs," Amy said. "You ate five bags on the plane."

"I was hungry!"

"I was trying to sleep! *Crunch crunch crunch!* Right in my ear. All night long."

"Guys? Can we focus?" Fiske asked, stifling a yawn. "Let's get to the hotel, shower, get something to eat, and then we can head to the bank."

"This is the cleanest airport I've ever seen," Dan said, registering the gleaming hallway and stainless steel handrails.

"Welcome to Switzerland," Fiske said. "Everything works."

They followed signs to the train that would take them to the main terminal. They hadn't checked any baggage. Amy and Dan were used to traveling light. All three had backpacks, and Fiske held a canvas tote bag with a guidebook and some newspapers.

They boarded the train with a crowd of other tired passengers. The train zipped through a concrete tunnel while a disembodied voice called out terminal information in several languages.

"Switzerland has four official languages," Fiske told them. "German, French, Italian, and Romansch. Most people speak English, too. But you'll hear more German in Zurich."

"Look, Amy," Dan said. "Heidi is blowing us a kiss."

Sure enough, a moving image flashed on the window. A woman in braids standing in an alpine meadow waved and leaned forward to blow them a kiss.

"Wow, look at that. I'd love to see the Alps," Amy said.

"We won't have time for that on this trip," Fiske said. "After the bank, it would be safest to leave the country. Tell you what; after we check in to the hotel, I'll take you to Café Schober for a second breakfast—they have the best hot chocolate in the world."

They exited the train at the main terminal and followed signs for baggage and taxis. "Wow, can't we stay and buy some chocolate?" Dan asked, his head swiveling as he took in the array of shops. "Or a watch?"

"Switzerland is known for its banks, too," Fiske said. "Let's try that instead."

As they reached the exit, they saw a driver in a thick wool coat and cap holding up a sign: SMITH.

"That's us," Fiske said.

"Smith?" Dan asked. "That's the best you can do?"

"Hey, I like an easy alias."

"Mr. Smith?" the driver asked crisply as they walked up. "Let me take your bags, sir. The car is right outside."

"No luggage," Fiske said. "We're ready to go."

They followed the driver to a black car parked with the other limousines and hired cars. Amy and Dan threw their backpacks inside the trunk, along with Fiske's.

"We'll be at the Widder Hotel in a few minutes, sir," the driver said.

"Fine, fine," Fiske said. The driver held the door, but Fiske suddenly staggered. He leaned on the frame of the car.

"You okay?" Dan asked him.

He wiped his forehead. "Just got dizzy for a minute. I forgot to take my medication on the plane."

"What m—" Dan started to ask, but Amy stepped on his foot. Something was wrong.

"You forgot again?" she said in concern.

"Could you get my pack?" Fiske asked the driver.

"Of course, sir."

As soon as the driver moved toward the rear of the car, Fiske jerked his head away from the car. The three of them leaped back on the curb and raced toward the taxi stand. Fiske signaled a cab that was just letting off a passenger. Urging them forward in a run, he sidestepped the exiting passenger and danced Dan and Amy into the backseat. He jumped in after them.

"Drive!" he barked to the driver.

"Of course. That is what one does in this kind of situation. But where, sir?"

"Anywhere! The Fraumünster! As quick as you can!" Fiske ordered.

"What just happened?" Dan exploded.

"I never gave the car company our hotel information," Fiske said.

The information sunk in slowly, like a footstep in mud.

"They know we're here," Amy said. She turned around and eyed the road behind them. It was full of black cars. It was impossible to tell if they were being followed.

Fiske leaned forward. "Take this exit!" he ordered the driver.

"Now?"

"NOW!" the three of them shouted.

The car swerved off the highway. Amy, Dan, and Fiske

all twisted around to look out the rear window. They saw a black car cross two lanes of traffic, trying to get to the exit, but with a squeal of tires and much honking from the other cars, it was forced to stay on the highway.

"There goes my green cashmere sweater," Amy said, thinking of the items in her backpack. It was the sweater Evan had complimented and now it was gone.

"You sound like Natalie Kabra," Dan said. "*I* lost my iPod. *That's* tragic!"

"At least we still have our cell phones," Amy said.

"Don't worry, I have my credit cards," Fiske said. "And a bag," he added with a grin, holding up the canvas tote. "We should go straight to the bank. We just bought ourselves some time. But it's running out." He leaned forward and spoke crisply to the driver. "Head toward Bahnhofstrasse, please."

●●●

Fiske drove the cabdriver crazy by making him turn corners, drive into parking lots and reverse out, and go blocks out of the way before they were sure they weren't being followed. The driver looked relieved when they finally exited the cab.

The bank was located on a swanky street with fashionable pedestrians and designer stores. Fiske, Amy, and Dan looked up at the gray stone building. Suddenly, they felt too disheveled and casual to venture inside. Dan and Amy were dressed in jeans and heavy parkas, and Fiske was wearing his usual black jeans, this time with a black knit cap and a peacoat.

"We look like we're going to rob the joint," Dan joked.

"What does a numbered account mean?" Amy asked Fiske.

"It means the name doesn't go on the paperwork," Fiske explained, "but it's not anonymous. The bank knows Grace Cahill. They're expecting us."

Inside, the floor was polished stone. An antique desk sat on a beautiful jewel-toned carpet. A man in a gray suit sat at the desk behind a computer. A security guard stood to the side.

"May I help you, sir?" The man's gaze coolly took in their standard American tourist attire. Fiske quickly removed his knit cap, but that made it worse. Serious hat hair made him look like a spooked gray cat.

"I'm here to access a numbered account."

The man pushed a keypad across the table. "Please enter the number, sir."

Fiske entered a number onto the keypad. The man looked at his screen. It took a moment but Amy was positive she heard the crack of ice melting as the man registered some serious money.

"Of course, sir. Welcome." He clicked a few keys. "For your protection, sir, may I see your passports?"

The three of them handed over their passports, and the man scanned them into the computer.

"You may enter." Behind him, double steel doors slid open.

A woman was already standing there, slender

and poised in a dark suit. Her gray hair was short and spiked, and her gaze was brisk and businesslike behind rectangular black glasses. She spoke with a slight German accent. "Mr. Cahill, welcome. I am Frau Bodner, private banker for Grace Cahill. We here at the bank were saddened to hear of her death."

"Thank you. This is Dan Cahill, Grace's grandson, and Amy Cahill, her granddaughter."

The gaze shifted to Amy. "She is on the account, along with you."

"Yes."

"I can conduct your business, but first, I'm so sorry to request this, but we do require retinal scans. Security is of course our first concern here."

"Of course."

The woman led them to a flat panel. Amy put her eye up to the screen. She heard a faint whirr, and she stepped away. Fiske did the same, then Dan.

"Now you're in our records. We can proceed."

Another door, this one of satiny wood, slid open. They were in a richly carpeted hallway with dark walnut paneling. At the end was a bank of elevators. Frau Bodner swiped her card at the elevator panel. The doors opened. She stood aside to let them enter, then followed, swiping the card again.

The elevator rose to the twentieth floor. Amy felt woozy. It seemed like yesterday she was doing her homework back in Attleboro and trying not to think about Evan. *Actually, it was yesterday*, she corrected herself. But now she was shooting up to a secure floor in a Swiss bank, chasing after an ancient ring. Another legacy from Grace, another task that her grandmother seemed to think they were capable of handling. Maybe they were only brave because Grace expected them to be.

The doors opened. This corridor was gray — gray walls, gray carpet, and stainless steel doors. Frau Bodner led them down the hallway to an ornate door with steel pieces twisted in an elaborate pattern that did not disguise the fact that they were security bars.

A guard stood outside, earpiece in place. She nodded at him, once again slid her security card through the slot, then pressed her eye against the retinal scanner. Then she punched in a code.

This place had more security checks than Fort Knox. Amy slid her wet palms on her jeans. Grace wasn't a high-tech-security kind of person. She relied on people she knew for years, like William MacIntyre, who worked in one of the oldest and stodgiest law firms in Boston. She couldn't picture her grandmother here. What would make her travel thousands of miles to this cold and forbidding place?

Something so precious she would go to any length to protect it.

"This way."

They followed Frau Bodner into another room, this one like an enormous safe. The guard followed. She punched in a number on a screen, and a wall of numbered boxes slid silently aside. Another wall of boxes slid forward. Frau Bodner walked to one of the boxes and motioned to Fiske. She placed her key in the lock, and Fiske placed his. They both turned the keys, and the box slid outward.

It was bigger than Amy had imagined, the size of a small overnight case, only narrower. It was made of metal. Frau Bodner carried the box to the far wall. A series of steel doors ran down its length. She swiped her card outside one of them.

They followed her inside the small room. There was a table, several chairs, and bottled water and glasses on a silver tray.

"You may take as long as you like," Frau Bodner said. "When you are finished, press this button. The security officer will alert me, and I'll usher you out."

Fiske thanked her, and she nodded and left, the door clicking shut behind her.

The box sat in the middle of the table. They stared at it.

"Wouldn't it be cool if it was full of priceless jewels?" Dan whispered. "Or gold bars?"

Amy eyed the box. "What are you, a pirate? We already have plenty of money."

"There's nothing like a couple of gold bars for authenticity, though. I could make one into a necklace. Jonah Wizard would be soooo way jealous. . . ."

Amy looked over at Dan. Was he babbling because he was nervous or because he was excited? It was almost like he was *enjoying* this. Didn't he want to be back in Attleboro, sitting in their living room? She sure did.

Fiske sat down in a chair, grabbed the box, and slid it toward himself. He took a breath, then opened it.

Amy leaned forward. The only thing in the box was an envelope addressed to Fiske in Grace's handwriting.

Fiske picked up the envelope, opened it, and took out a sheet of paper. He placed it flat on the table so that they could all read it at the same time.

> Baby Brother,
>
> Compass points — our lives together. We grew. We traveled. We grew apart. We came together.
>
> Childhood memory still binds us. Do you remember how we roasted potatoes in the fire? Our European birthdays — yours, mine. Up, down.
>
> The meadows and the peaks — we saw it all.
>
> Now I ask you to do one last thing. Pass it on. The circle of devotion never ends.
>
> All my yearning . . . now comes to this. Keep it close.
>
> G

"Amy," Dan said, poking her. "Do us a favor? Don't go all emo on us."

"I'm not crying," Amy said, dabbing at her eyes. "But the note . . . it's so sad."

Fiske looked in the box again. He tapped at it. "But where's the ring?"

They bent over the paper again. Amy reached out

and touched it. Seeing Grace's handwriting always made her choke up.

"'The circle of devotion,'" she whispered.

Suddenly, Dan snorted.

Amy looked up, annoyed. "Don't get all sarcastic. It's beautiful."

"It's sappy," Dan said. "And Grace wasn't sappy."

Amy opened her mouth to protest, but Fiske looked at Dan, his blue eyes keen. "He's right. Go on, Dan."

Dan stared down at the paper. "This is a code. Grace didn't write like this, all poetic and sentimental. She said what she meant. 'All my yearning'? Give me a break!"

"It's the ring!" Amy burst out. "The circle of devotion!"

"Look at the first letters of 'all my yearning,'" Fiske said. "They're slightly darker."

"'A M Y,'" Dan read. He looked over at Amy. "Oh, no, not again!"

Amy sniffed as a tear rolled down her cheek. "'*Amy* now comes to this,'" she read. "That's what she meant."

"You're the next Madrigal to protect the ring," Fiske said.

"Yeah," Dan said. "We just have to find it."

"'Compass points,'" Fiske murmured. "Why—" Suddenly, he stopped when a light flashed red and began to blink. A siren wailed behind the door.

They heard a brisk knock at the door, and it opened to reveal the security guard. "Excuse me," he said with a German accent. "Armed gunmen have broken into the bank. We must leave immediately!"

●●●●●

Thieves . . . or Vespers?

Either scenario wasn't good, Dan decided.

"Hurry!" the guard said as Fiske stuffed the paper in his pocket and closed the box.

When they reached the corridor, they turned toward the elevator, but the guard spoke quickly. "No! There is another elevator that can bring us to the underground garage." He spoke rapidly in German into his radio.

They ran down the corridor. Dan felt his heart banging against his chest. It was like a weird flashback to the Clue hunt. Only they weren't being chased by Cahills but by strangers with guns. He wasn't sure if it was incredibly cool or just incredibly scary.

All he knew was that he wasn't bored.

And *that* was a weirdly satisfying feeling.

The security guard moved quickly and efficiently. He swiped his card at the elevator bank but his eyes darted back down the corridor. He checked his belt, nervously touching the gun holster and a device that might have held pepper spray. Dan hoped it wasn't his first day.

The elevator doors opened and they hurried inside. The guard reached out to hit the button for the garage.

As he did, his cuff slid up, and Dan saw part of a tattoo on the inside of his wrist.

Something fluttered in his memory. As the elevator whooshed downward, he searched for it. The inked image was a symbol of something . . . but what?

I know it, I know it, I know it . . .

Some ancient symbol he'd seen in China? A strange character he'd glimpsed in Japan or Korea? Or what about some ancient Egyptian god?

Whatever it was, it was making him uneasy.

"This is crazy!" he burst out. "What if they're down there, waiting for us?" Amy looked at him strangely as he turned into a freakazoid. "You can't protect us!" he shouted, grabbing at the guard's arm.

"Chill, it's under control!" the guard said irritably as he shook him off.

Chill? Would a Swiss guy say that?

This time the cuff slid farther back. And Dan was staring into the goofy face of Dinger, the purple triceratops that was the mascot of the Colorado Rockies baseball team.

Why would a German-accented Swiss security guard have a tattoo like that?

The elevator floors ticked off. Dan wrestled with his instincts. The guy could have gone to college in the States. But it wasn't adding up.

Dan shot a look at Amy, a look that said *something about this isn't right.*

Her eyes went wide. The elevator was shooting

down to the parking garage, and he had a feeling that when the doors opened, they wouldn't be met with a parade.

Well, if the guy *was* a security guard, he'd just have to forgive him.

Dan inclined his head toward the red emergency stop button. Amy nodded. He grabbed the tote bag from Fiske and upended it. The guidebook thumped to the floor, distracting the guard just as Amy leaped forward and hit the stop button.

The elevator jerked to a halt. They all staggered. Dan had been waiting for just that. He slipped the tote bag over the guard's head. He heard the muffled cry of the guard, but he had exactly one instant of surprise to work with, and he used it. He smashed his foot into the back of the guard's knee, and the guy lost his balance and fell on his knees, letting out a howl. He reached out blindly and with one hand tried to get the canvas bag off his head, but with the other he grabbed Dan by the throat . . . and squeezed.

Dan clawed at the hand. He felt enormous pressure and enormous pain. He saw Amy slamming her fists against the guard. It was like hitting a mountain.

Fiske doubled over. Was he hurt? Then he drove downward, slamming a tightly rolled newspaper into the back of the guard's neck. To Dan's amazement, the guard hit the floor. The pressure on his throat eased.

"Whoa, dude!" Dan choked. "Are you a CIA agent in disguise?"

"Amazing the things you learn in the Cahill family," Fiske said, sitting down on top of the guard. "Now, can you tell me what's up?"

"I think he's a Vesper." Quickly, Dan explained about the tattoo and how the guy had said "chill." It sounded lame suddenly, with an unconscious man lying on the floor.

Fiske looked up at Amy. "Amy, can you hit a floor? Anything high will do. We'd better get off this elevator."

Amy hit the top floor. When the elevator began to move, Fiske swiftly reached down and took the gun.

"Awesome," Dan breathed.

Then Fiske took the pepper spray and waited until the doors opened. He lifted a bit of the tote bag, sprayed it in the guy's face, and walked out. "He'll have a good cry when he comes to."

Amy reached back into the elevator and punched every floor on the panel. It would be a long trip down.

"I hope you're right," Amy said to Dan.

"He's right," Fiske said. "It adds up. He made a mistake in German—he used *du* instead of *Sie* when he spoke into that transmitter. Dan just has faster reactions than I do." Dan grinned, and he and Fiske gently knocked their knuckles together.

The gray-carpeted hall was empty. They walked cautiously past a suite of offices. To their surprise, they could see people working quietly.

"What's going on?" Amy whispered. "Don't they know what's happening?"

"Maybe the alarm malfunctioned," Dan said.

"This is an executive floor," Fiske said, peering at the nameplates. "This guy is a vice president."

"And here's the president of the bank," Dan said. "We might as well go straight to the top."

They opened the door and walked in. Two assistants sat at twin desks on either side of a double door with gigantic steel knobs. Both men were dressed in gray suits. Both wore their blond hair cropped short. Enormous paintings in cool tones of silver and gray hung on the walls. The only splotch of color was the deep blue of Lake Zurich below.

"May I help you?" The man on the left addressed them.

The guy looked perfectly calm. This was getting weirder and weirder.

"I'm Fiske Cahill, an account holder here. We were just going through our safe-deposit box when a guard told us there were armed thieves in the bank—"

"Who were on their way up to that floor—" Dan interrupted.

"And then we realized he was one of them, so we wrestled him to the floor—"

Both assistants' eyes were on them now.

"We have received no security alerts," the first one said. He primly adjusted his silver-framed glasses.

Fiske took out the gun and slammed it on the desk. That got their attention.

"I think this belongs to the bank," he said.

The silver-framed glasses guy licked his lips. "I think you'd better see Herr Duber."

"Good call," Fiske said.

Within seconds, the door opened, and a tall, gray-haired man nodded at them. He, too, seemed fashioned of metal. Silver hair, silver glasses, steel-gray eyes.

"What is it, Bruno?" he asked testily.

The blond man in the glasses gestured at them and shrugged, as if to say he wasn't responsible for the three crazy Americans in front of him.

"They have a story about a bank heist, like an American film." He gave a disdainful smile.

"It's not a *story*," Dan said furiously.

Herr Duber frowned. "Why don't you start at the beginning?"

It took another few minutes for them to spill out the story to Herr Duber. He immediately called security. He frowned as he listened, then said something in German and replaced the receiver. "There are no armed intruders in the bank."

Fiske looked at Dan and Amy. "But we heard a siren!" Amy cried.

"We don't have a siren," Herr Duber said. "We have a silent alarm."

"He must have pressed something against the door," Amy murmured.

"And that flashing red light?" Dan wondered. "He could have stuck it up there and activated it with a remote."

"Something's going on," Fiske said. "I'd think you'd want to get to the bottom of it."

"I agree, Mr. Cahill. Please come with me," Herr Duber said.

He led them down the corridor. It opened into another corridor, with no gray carpet, no art on the walls. Herr Duber swiped a card outside the first door to the left and ushered them inside.

Several guards sat glued to banks of monitors, not even turning to greet them.

They waited while Herr Duber spoke briefly to a man in a dark suit, gesturing at them. They felt the man's hard gaze on them. He turned and spoke to one of the men at the monitors. Then he leaned in, watching carefully.

Fiske, Amy, and Dan walked over. They looked at the grainy gray image of an elevator.

"You see the timer there?" Herr Duber said, pointing. "You said you took the service elevator, the one to the garage? It's been empty for an hour."

"That isn't possible," Amy murmured.

"What about the security officer?" Fiske asked.

"His shift ended ten minutes ago," the man in the dark suit said. "He punched out and left."

"This is Herr Moser, chief of security," Herr Duber explained.

"The guard tricked us," Dan said. "And you. Can't you see? He tampered with the cameras!"

"So you say," Moser said.

"You have the items in your safe-deposit box, correct?" Herr Duber broke in. "So nothing is missing. We have checked the entire area. We don't allow surveillance cameras in the viewing room, of course," he added. "For complete privacy."

"It doesn't matter that nothing is missing," Fiske said. "There was a security breach. If I were you, I'd call the police."

"But nothing has been stolen." Moser's mouth was a thin line. "We prefer to handle this internally."

"What about the security officer?" Fiske asked.

"I assure you, all employees undergo background checks—"

"Can we see the surveillance tape from outside the safe-deposit area?"

The guard hit a few keys on the computer. They saw the timer running along the bottom of the image. There was the security guard, standing. Standing. Standing.

"That's Bachmann," Moser said. "He's new. Impeccable resume."

"Yeah, except for the criminal activity part," Dan said. "Look at the running clock. We were leaving the area less than ten minutes ago and the corridor is empty. This is bogus!"

"This word I don't know—bogus." Moser shot him a glance that clearly said he thought he was dealing with The Family Crazypants.

"If I were you," Dan said, "I'd double-check the backgrounds of every single employee in this bank. This guy Bachmann couldn't have done this on his own."

The security chief looked at him, and the mask of politeness slipped. "I am not accustomed to taking advice from little boys."

Dan was ready to kick him, but Fiske put a hand on his shoulder. "Dude," he said. "It's time to start."

● ● ●

They left the bank by the side entrance and quickly jumped into a taxi. Fiske told the driver to take a scenic ride around the lake.

"They could be tailing us right now," Amy said with a shiver.

"I don't think so," Fiske said. He'd been checking behind them since they'd gotten into the car.

"I say we get the jump on them," Dan said.

"How?" Amy asked.

Dan reached into the pocket of his parka. He held out a nylon wallet on his palm. "I picked the guard's pocket before we left the elevator. Just call me Lightfinger Dan."

"The guy was unconscious," Amy said.

"Yeah, but my moves were soooo smooth," Dan said.

They leaned forward expectantly as Dan emptied the wallet, but all it held was a few crumpled Swiss francs and an ID for Maxwell Bachmann.

Dan tossed the ID aside in disappointment. "Definitely a fake. This doesn't tell us anything."

Fiske picked it up off the seat. "Not necessarily."

He balanced the picture ID on his knee, then snapped a few photos of it with his phone. "I'll send this to Erasmus. He's got a database of possible Vespers in his head."

"Don't forget to tell him about the tattoo," Dan said.

Fiske nodded as he rapidly punched the information into his phone.

The face of the Vesper stared up at Dan. The guy looked like a student, not a criminal master mind. He would have passed him on the street without a second look.

Fiske's phone buzzed. He held it up so that they could read the message.

CASPER WYOMING VERY DANGEROUS. DO NOT APPROACH.

"Casper, Wyoming?" Dan asked incredulously. We're nowhere near it."

"It's not a city," Fiske said. "It's a name."

"'Very dangerous,'" Amy repeated. "Well, at least he doesn't know where we are. Or where we're going."

"Do we? Dan asked.

"We do," Fiske told them. "I figured out what Grace was trying to tell me. It's so obvious I didn't see it."

"So where are we going?" Amy asked.

"Zermatt, Switzerland," Fiske announced. "You'll get to see the Alps after all!"

•••••

As the sleek, comfortable train rocketed through the picturesque countryside, Fiske spread Grace's note on his lap and settled his reading glasses on his nose.

"'Compass points,'" he said. "It was driving me crazy. Compass points refers to the Matterhorn."

"Isn't that the ride at Disneyland?" Dan asked.

"Exactly," Fiske said. "And it's based on the mountain in Switzerland. It has four faces, each oriented in a different direction—north, south—"

"—east, west," Amy finished. "Compass points. But I still don't get how you figured out it was the mountain."

"*Matte* means *meadow* in German, and *horn* means *peak*. That was the other clue, in case I didn't get 'compass points.' Our parents owned a chalet in Zermatt," Fiske said. "Grace and Beatrice went there when they were young. Then Father died, and somehow it was never sold. Then, when I dropped out of college . . . which, by the way, you should never do—" He interrupted himself, looking at them over his glasses.

Dan rolled his eyes at Amy. "Thanks for the lecture, Uncle Fiske, but can you get to the point?"

"After I dropped out, Grace treated me to a trip to Europe. One of the stops was the chalet. She had never gone back before. I think it reminded her too much of happier days. Anyway, we had our last visit together for what turned out to be . . . a very long time. I was afraid of what Grace thought of me. I thought she'd call me a wimp. Because I wanted out. Out of the whole Cahill family, out of the games and the betrayals and the stupid petty jealousies . . . The rest of the Cahills thought I was weak because I didn't want to play."

Amy and Dan sat straight and still. Fiske had never talked much about his life. He had told them how he'd dropped out and "bummed around the world" for years. He'd never explained, and they'd never asked.

"I knew Grace wanted me to help her. I knew she needed me to watch her back. But she did a generous thing. She told me to go and never come back. She told me to get lost."

"Wow, I tell Amy to get lost all the time," Dan said. "It never works."

"She meant *get lost,* really lose myself so that the Cahills could never find me. She said that one day they'd forget about me because I wasn't useful anymore. She was right about that, by the way. But back then, she gave me her blessing. And a Swiss bank account," he added, smiling. "Grace was always practical. So I got lost. I lived in Thailand for a while, New Zealand, Bali . . . settled in Portugal. We were in touch, would see each other from time to time. And when she called me home I booked my flight that same day. I knew she was dying. She didn't have to tell me."

There was a short silence. Amy felt the slight swaying of the train and blinked at the green meadows floating by outside the window. That bond — sister and brother — had held strong. It didn't matter that Fiske had gone underground. Grace had made sure he was all right.

"It was Grace who raised me. I was her baby. So the fact that she let me go" — Fiske cleared his throat — "was the most generous act she could do."

Dan looked down at the note. "So what about potatoes?"

"That's the part that's confusing," Fiske said. "We roasted potatoes in the fire, but not at the chalet. We certainly didn't do it on every birthday."

"Maybe the point isn't the potatoes," Amy said. "Maybe it's the fireplace."

Fiske nodded. "The chalet has a big fireplace — the ring could be hidden there. You know, in Grace's last days, she told me I could do anything I wanted with what was left — the mansion, the Nantucket house, the paintings, the books — but I was never to sell the chalet, or even modernize it or change it in any way. She had hired a local woman as a caretaker for it, so it was well tended. I was to pass it to Amy. I didn't understand it at the time. I thought maybe you were a terrific skier or something, Amy."

"If you count falling down on the bunny slope," Amy said with a grin. She'd been skiing in Massachusetts, but she was no expert. She frowned. "So the ring must be there."

This was the part of the Clue hunt that she'd liked — figuring out puzzles. She could do without the near-escapes.

They thought over it for a while, but the slight sway of the train and the lack of sleep from the night before acted on all of them. Amy saw Fiske place her jacket gently over her as she drifted off into sleep.

●●●●●

They woke up in time to change trains and then boarded a smaller, red railcar with big observation windows. They climbed through the mountains, through meadows deep with snow and storybook houses that looked like the Von Trapp family was inside singing "My Favorite Things."

As they chugged the last miles toward Zermatt, they couldn't help but gasp when the Matterhorn came into view, looming sharp and clear against the blue sky.

"It's amazing," Amy said.

"It's over fourteen thousand feet high," Fiske said.

"Fourteen thousand, six hundred and ninety-two, actually," Amy said.

"It's not as hard to climb as it used to be," Fiske said, "but the cemetery has quite a few graves of climbers. Two students from Cambridge University were lost on the mountain back in the fifties. They found their bodies thirty years later."

Dan shuddered. "That's pretty harsh."

"It's a harsh mountain. It also has the highest cable car station in Europe," Fiske went on. "But I think we'll stay closer to the ground. As soon as we, uh, collect the package, we should think about moving on. We can pretty much bet that Casper Wyoming isn't working alone."

The train glided into the station. They filed out with the other passengers, who were searching for ski equipment and luggage.

"There are no cars in Zermatt," Fiske explained. "They have electric taxis, funicular railways, and a tram. And, of course, all the cable cars. I e-mailed Frau Weiser, and she said the place will be ready for us."

The resort town of Zermatt was bustling with skiers and shoppers. Many of the pedestrians clomped around in ski boots, some carrying their skis. The main street, the Bahnhofstrasse, was lined with exclusive shops filled with designer ski clothes, jewelry stores with thick, heavy gold watches, and bakery windows stuffed with pastries.

"We can take the funicular railway up to the chalet," Fiske said. "It's a short walk from the stop."

The railway dropped them off at the entrance to a trail leading upward. Fiske pointed to the left. "You see over there? You can ski out of the chalet right to the cable car stop that takes you up the mountain."

They trudged through the snow, glad they'd all worn their winterized boots. A small chalet lay ahead, surrounded by snowy pines. They stamped their boots on the front walk to remove the snow and walked inside.

The interior was cold and still. "Guess the heat hasn't had a chance to warm up the place," Fiske said. "It's been empty a long time."

A massive fireplace took up most of one wall. The furniture was worn and comfortable, and the view was spectacular. Below were the rooftops of Zermatt, and the mountains rose up all around them.

"Props to Frau Weiser!" Dan called from the kitchen. "She left us chocolate!"

Fiske and Amy stood by the fireplace. Dan joined them, munching on chocolate. They stared at the blackened bricks as though they would give up their secret.

"Birthdays," Amy murmured. She stripped off her gloves and stuck them in her pocket, but she kept her parka on. "Grace's birthday, your birthday." She knelt down by the fireplace. "If we were roasting potatoes, we'd have to be right here . . . look!" she said excitedly. "There's a scratch on this brick—it looks like an M!"

Fiske and Dan bent down to look. "Madrigals," Fiske said.

Dan nodded. "So, birthdays . . ."

"That's it! Grace said up, then down," Amy said. "We take the numbers of your birthdays, and count the bricks. Grace was born on December twenty-fourth, so that's month twelve, on the twenty-fourth, so we count twelve up, and then twenty-four down. We leave out the birth year because we'd be all the way up the chimney." Amy went up the bricks, counting as she went. "Now we go down, for your birthday, August ninth, so that's eight up and then nine down. . . ."

Amy stopped at a brick. She tapped it with a fingernail, then pulled at it. "It's really stuck. Do we have tools?"

Dan took the key off the table where Fiske had left it. He knelt next to Amy and pried at the brick. "We need something sharper. We have to scrape away all the mortar."

Fiske shook his head. "I don't know about this. It seems to me that the brick should be loose, so that it would be relatively easy to pry out."

"Unless we're totally wrong about everything," Dan said.

Amy rocked back on her heels. "Wait a second. Didn't Grace say 'our birthdays in Europe' or something like that?"

"She said 'our European birthdays,'" Dan corrected.

"People write dates in Europe differently," Amy said. "They put the day first, then the month. We do the month first in the US. So . . ."

"So we need to count the birth *day*, then the month," Fiske finished.

Amy went back to the brick with the letter M. This time she counted twenty-four up and twelve down, then nine up and eight down. She put her hand on the brick and it moved in her hand. "It's loose!" she cried.

"Here." Dan handed her the key.

She slid it along the side. "I think I can get it. . . ." She pried the brick loose and lifted it out of the floor. She held her breath as she reached into the space and withdrew a small silk pouch.

It was easy to untie the knot. She upended the pouch and shook it. The ring dropped into her palm.

It was old, worn, and dull. She could just make out some characters or symbols on it. She held it up. "It doesn't look like much." She slipped it on her third finger, but it was too loose, so she pushed it on her thumb.

"We actually found it," Dan said, shaking his head. "Thanks, Grace!"

Amy turned the ring on her thumb. Grace had given her this charge, and she had to protect it, even though she didn't know why. What should she do now? Wear it? Bring it to another bank? Hide it somewhere safe? Where? It had remained under that brick for a long time. Maybe she should just put it back.

As her gaze rested on the floor, she slowly became aware that a stain was spreading out from underneath a closet door. A dark red pool . . .

"Uncle Fiske?" she whispered. "Over there . . ."

Fiske turned, and she saw him swallow. "Wait in the kitchen, you two," he said.

But they stayed right where they were as he went to the closet door and opened it.

Amy cried out as a woman fell heavily out onto the floor. Blood dripped from a wound on her forehead.

Amy started forward, but a noise made her turn. Casper Wyoming was heading down the stairs toward them.

Fiske reacted first. He leaped forward to put himself between Casper and Amy and Dan.

"Run!" he shouted to them.

Dan couldn't seem to move. His mind heard the command, but his body was frozen.

Fiske landed a kick into Casper's midsection, then twisted to attempt an uppercut to his jaw, but Casper dodged it. Dan and Amy watched in horror as Casper picked Fiske up like a dry piece of kindling and heaved him against the wall. It all happened so fast. Dan heard Amy scream "NO!" as Fiske hit the wall with a terrible noise. His face contorted in pain as he landed awkwardly on his ankle and went down.

But Casper wasn't interested in Fiske. He advanced on them, his eyes on Amy's thumb. Amy stood frozen, watching Casper approach.

Purpose pumped through Dan's body again. He yanked on Amy's arm, pulling her away as Fiske suddenly lunged toward Casper from the floor. He grabbed Casper's ankle, but Casper kicked him viciously. Fiske grunted but managed to hold on.

"Go," he said through his teeth, his steel-blue gaze clouded with pain but still full of force.

It gave them just enough time. They ran out through the back door, straight down a ramp. *You can ski right to the cable car stop,* Fiske had said. They raced down the snowy incline, trying not to slip. Casper burst out of the house behind them.

"Kids!" Casper yelled. "Give it up! I only want the ring! I won't hurt you."

"Does he think we're stupid?" Amy muttered. She took Dan's hand and yanked him off the path. Dan saw immediately what she was thinking. They could have an advantage here—Casper might not know where the cable car stop was.

"Where—" Amy asked.

Dan recalled it perfectly, like a picture in his head. . . . Fiske pointing up the mountain, the high lines of the cables, the cable car stop, a concrete modern structure jutting out over the slope. No doubt there would be people there, too. "This way."

He took the lead and they raced down the slope, dodging the pines. The afternoon was waning. If they could get aboard the cable car, they could lose themselves among the skiers trying to fit in a last run. Then they could get down the mountain on another car. It wasn't much, but it was their best shot.

Almost there. Casper wasn't wearing boots, so he kept slipping and sliding and cursing his way through the trees. "He's not exactly Outdoor Dude," Dan said. He could feel his lungs squeezing, but he didn't want Amy to know he was out of breath. He just needed one last burst of energy. Then he could use his inhaler. The station was ahead. A cable car was approaching. They could make it.

They burst into the station. A set of turnstiles stood between them and the cable car. Skiers in front of them had some sort of electronic card that got them through. Some of them waved the card, and others just thrust out a hip and the turnstile beeped and let them pass.

Amy and Dan exchanged glances. There was no time. Casper was just coming into the station, his jeans wet with snow. They vaulted over the turnstiles and catapulted themselves into the car just as the doors were closing.

"You have to pay!" the cable car operator scolded them as the car lurched forward.

Outside on the platform, Casper hauled off and punched a concrete column.

Amy put on her most contrite look. "Our parents have the lift passes!" she said. "We got separated and we don't have any money! They'll be up at the top, waiting for us."

Dan took out his inhaler and took a deep hit. He felt his lungs expand and he got a full breath. He tried to look honest and sickly at the same time.

"All right, all right," the operator said. "You'll have to find them and pay when we get there, then."

They sidled over and tried to lose themselves among the dozen skiers who were going up for a last run.

"Did you see that?" Dan muttered. "The dude punched *concrete*."

"I hope Fiske is okay."

"Look—there's Casper." They could just see him below on the slope as he took out a cell phone. "We beat you, sucker!" Dan whispered.

"For now," Amy said. "Who is he calling? The Vespers must know about Grace's chalet. We were sure no one was following us back in Zurich."

"At least we have time to figure out what to do next," Dan said. "He can't beat us up the mountain."

The cable car soared smoothly up the mountain, gaining height as it went. Soon they were hundreds of feet above the snow. The skiers laughed and chatted in several languages. A man pointed out a ski run to his wife.

Amy closed her eyes. "I didn't expect it to be so . . . high."

Dan looked out over the breathtaking vista. They were past the tree line now, and he could make out skiers on the trails, tiny dots that zigged and zagged.

He was glad that he and Amy were still wearing their parkas. It was cold up here, and the wind rattled the car.

"We left Fiske and that poor woman down there. Do you think she's dead?" Amy whispered, her face pale.

"No," Dan said. But the truth was, he wasn't sure. He took another discreet puff on his inhaler. His heartbeat was slowing down, but he was having trouble focusing.

At first this had seemed so cool, to be back on the run, outwitting the bad guys. But the Vespers—he didn't know these guys at all, and that scared him. He could still hear the sickening *thunk* of Fiske's head hitting the wall. Casper had treated Fiske like an insect, something in his way to be squashed under his shoe. The look in his eyes . . . it was as though Fiske were something less than human.

He wasn't ready to get plunged back into this. He wasn't ready at all.

But he couldn't tell his sister that. She'd worry even more than she was worrying now.

Amy pressed closer to the glass. She pointed down the mountain. "Take a look at that helicopter."

A copter was heading across the sky, casting a shadow on the pristine white snow.

It powered closer, its propeller whirring. They could see the pilot now, and a man sitting in the seat next to him.

"They're arguing," Amy said.

"Look. That copter is getting awfully close," one of the women in the car said nervously to her companion.

Someone else said something in French. The cable car operator looked out and frowned. He spoke into his headset.

Suddenly, the passenger in the helicopter lunged forward. They saw the pilot jerk violently backward.

"He has a gun!" someone yelled.

The passenger began to push the pilot out of the seat. The helicopter tilted crazily.

An American man yelled, "Call the authorities!"

"He shot the pilot!" his wife screamed.

The pilot, they saw, was fighting for his life.

Helplessly, they watched as the passenger clubbed the pilot with the butt of the gun. He hung on to his seat while the passenger pushed him toward the open door. Someone next to Dan hammered on the glass of the cable car and cried out something in German.

Then they all screamed with one voice as the passenger reared back and kicked the pilot halfway out the open door. The pilot gripped the side of the helicopter, but with one brutal thrust the passenger pushed him off. They screamed in horror as the pilot's body fell, gaining velocity as he went down, until he was lost to sight.

Someone sobbed. The cable car was a babble of voices in different languages, calling out in anguish.

Dan swallowed quickly. He felt sick. Sweat broke out on his forehead. Amy looked at him, her eyes wide with horror.

"I've called the police," the operator shouted. He repeated the phrase in German and Italian.

Amy had turned back to the window. "It's not over," she whispered.

The passenger was now piloting the helicopter. It was heading straight for the cable car. Instinctively, everyone moved away from it, and the car lurched crazily to one side. Several people screamed.

"Stay calm!" the operator yelled. "Keep the car stable! The police are on their way!"

Dan cast a quick look up the mountain. They were far away from the top, and the drop must be hundreds of feet down. Now he could see the passenger's face. He felt the shock of recognition. It was the bank president's assistant, the one in the silver glasses. "It's Bruno!" he told Amy. "The guy from the bank who dissed us. He's a Vesper."

Amy was pale and glassy-eyed. "He's going to cut the cables."

Dan looked at her in alarm, then at the helicopter. It was higher than the cable car now and tilted to one side. The whirring blades were getting closer and closer. So close he could see the intent expression on the Vesper's face, the way his gaze stayed on the cables above.

"He can't—" Dan started, then swallowed. If the guy was trying to scare them, he was coming awfully close.

Screams erupted throughout the cabin. Instinctively, everyone moved back, and the car rocked again. Dan hung on to Amy as the helicopter loomed in their vision, Bruno's black-gloved hands steady on the controls.

Then a terrible shrieking sound resounded through the cabin, and the cable gave way. The car lurched, and some of the passengers were slammed to the floor. They began to slide toward the closed doors. Dan and Amy barely stayed on their feet. Screams filled the cabin.

"What's happening?" someone yelled in terror.

"We're all right!" the operator shouted above the screams. "We can't fall! There's one cable left. We're all right! We're all right," he kept repeating in English, then French, then Italian, then German, as though by saying it over and over it would make it real. But there was a sheen of perspiration on his face, and Dan could see fear in his eyes.

"He's coming back again!" a man shouted.

Amy took Dan's hand. He knew now what Amy had already guessed. The Vesper wasn't trying to scare them. He was going to kill them.

The whirring blades angled to the left, ready to cut the final cable and send them plunging to their death.

●●●●●

It's going to end here, like this?

The formula was in his head, the formula that could make him the most powerful person in the world. They had decided months ago that it was too dangerous to exist. Too dangerous to ingest.

But if he had done it, if he had taken it, could he have dispatched Casper Wyoming back in the chalet? He would have had the strength of a Tomas. If he'd had the cunning of a Lucian, would he have seen ahead and baited a trap instead of walking into one? If he'd thought more creatively, like a Janus, would he have come up with another way to escape, instead of climbing aboard a death trap? If he'd had the inventiveness of an Ekaterina, could he now figure out a way to get the cable car moving and away from this madman in a copter?

If I had it all—every power—could I have escaped this moment?

Dan faced the helicopter. He hadn't learned not to be afraid, but he had learned that turning away was not an option. He wanted the last thing he saw to be that guy's face, so the Vespers would know that Dan Cahill hadn't been scared. The terror that gripped him—his enemy would not see it.

"Polizia!" someone yelled.

Someone else was sobbing as the police helicopter flew at terrific speed toward the rogue helicopter. Dan could see Bruno's furious face as he dipped his copter sharply to the right and zoomed away, with the police in pursuit.

A few people were crying. The American man hugged his wife and rocked her from side to side. A tall German skier gave a short, strangled laugh. Relief made them all giddy for a moment. Until they remembered that they were still dangling over a staggering drop on only one cable.

"The rescue helicopter is on its way," the operator said. "We should see it in a moment."

"And then what?" Amy asked. "How will they fix the cable?"

The operator looked at her kindly. "They can't fix it," he said. "They're going to airlift us out."

"Air—airlift?"

"A rescue worker will be lowered by cable from the helicopter and he'll take one group out at a time. Don't worry, they are very good at their jobs," the operator said.

Dan suddenly realized that he was freezing. The

car wasn't heated, and condensation was beginning to build on the windows and ice over. It was difficult to see out now. Which was probably a good thing, being that Amy was a weenie about heights.

"Did they catch the helicopter pilot?" Dan asked the operator.

He shook his head. "Not yet. They'll get him."

Soon they heard the whirring of the blades. They could just glimpse the rescue helicopter approaching. Dangling at the end of a long cable was a rescue worker in a red parka. The helicopter flew higher, and they felt the slight bump as the rescue worker landed against the cable car. A second later the doors opened, and he swung in.

The noise of the copter was loud in their ears. He motioned to the man and wife close to him, and then to Dan and Amy. Slings were attached to the cable, and the man and his wife were already slipping into them.

"I have to sit in that and be towed in midair?" Amy asked. Her face looked terror stricken. "Dan, I can't do this."

"Are you kidding me? Of course you can. You've been on the top of Mount Everest! This is *cake.*" He didn't like the look on Amy's face. His sister was mad-brave when she was in the moment. It was the waiting that did her in.

"Come on." He urged her forward. "Can this be any worse than the time I made you jump off the balcony in that Cairo museum?"

Amy laughed weakly, but she moved forward and sat gingerly in the contraption. The rescue worker snapped her in.

Dan stepped into the sling.

"Ready?" the rescue worker shouted.

Everyone else nodded, and Amy's weak "Not really" was swallowed by the rush of wind as they stepped off the cable car into midair.

Dan felt the jolt of the cable and the blast of cold air in his face. Clouds were building in layers around the mountain, and the tiny pellets of snow striking his cheeks felt like ice. They swung at the bottom of the cable as the helicopter started down the mountain. Dan looked down and gulped. Amy kept her eyes closed.

They were probably in the air for about five minutes or so, but it felt longer. Finally, he saw far below a cluster of rescue workers clad in red parkas standing in a clearing near an alpine hut. The helicopter flew lower and lower, and he saw them waiting, arms outstretched. The helicopter hovered above, and in seconds, a rescuer had grabbed his legs. He almost toppled onto the guy. Now that relief was coursing through him, his muscles felt like slush.

"Are you okay?" the rescuer asked.

Dan nodded, even though he wasn't sure. Would the guy think he was crazy if he kissed the ground? He decided to skip it.

He could see now that the hut was bigger than he'd thought, and was a small restaurant. Skiers sat inside, most of them sipping at hot drinks while they watched the rescue operations. Some of them were in their stocking feet. It was odd to come back to a world where people sat around, warm and comfortable in their socks, eating soup, while he'd almost been turned into Dan Jam, smashed into goo on a mountainside.

He walked on unsteady legs toward Amy, who was already sitting on a bench, a mug of soup in her hands. Next to her, skis had been planted in the snow and were sticking straight up like a small forest. Snow boots were piled on a mat. There was a jumble of goggles in a basket.

Dan took the offered cup from a rescue worker and tasted the best soup of his life. Everything looked so sharp and clear—the blue shadows on the snow, the crazy clouds, the creamy ceramic sheen of the cup.

"You can go inside and warm up, if you wish," the rescue guy said. "Do you see the person talking to the couple over there? He is going to come over here and talk to you as well—he is a medic. You don't appear to be in shock, but we must check. Then you may take the tram down the mountain. There are escorts waiting."

"Thanks." Dan sank down next to Amy. "That was close," he said.

Amy turned to him. "We almost died, Dan. We really almost did this time." She shook her head. "I thought all this . . . was over. Is it ever going to be over?"

Dan didn't want to answer that question. Because they both knew the answer was *no*.

"We should call Fiske. But I don't have a signal," Amy said, snapping her phone closed. She scanned the area. "Casper Wyoming could be anywhere. Not to mention the other guy. We should get off the mountain. Didn't that guy say a rescue worker would escort us down? That's our best bet."

Dan didn't answer. He was studying the rescue worker who stood waiting patiently by the tram station. He was dressed in the same red jacket the other rescuers wore, his fleece cap pulled down to his eyebrows and a pair of goggles obscuring most of his face. Something about him was familiar, and not in a good way.

The worker patted his parka pocket for a minute. Like he was making sure something was there. *Like a weapon.*

He turned his back and spoke quickly to Amy. "Don't look, but that rescue guy is our friend Casper. He's waiting by the tram."

Amy's eyes widened. "What should we do? Should we tell someone?"

"Tell them what? That we're protecting an ancient ring? Or that there's this secret society called the Vespers?"

"I guess not. But we have to get down this mountain." Amy glanced over at the skis. "And there's only one way."

●●●

Within minutes, they were schussing down the slope.

The cloud cover was thicker, and the snow was falling more steadily now. Amy and Dan weren't experts, but luckily the run wasn't too steep . . . yet. They made good time down the mountain. Far below, they could see the lights of Zermatt beginning to twinkle on.

All they could hear was the *schuss, schuss* of their skis. Once in a while a skier would pass them, going down straight and fast.

Amy gave a quick glance behind. Her heart sank when she saw a skier in a red parka heading off from the hut. To her dismay, a skier clad in navy kept up the pace next to him. "Bad news—they're both behind us," she told Dan. "Bruno must have gotten away. And here's the other bad news—they look like experienced skiers."

"Apparently Casper *is* Outdoor Dude," Dan said through gritted teeth.

"We have to go off the trail. They have the advantage if we go straight downhill. They're much faster."

"I'm right behind you," Dan said.

Amy skied off the trail. The snow was icy and bumpy. She gripped her poles. It would be a disaster if one of them fell. She tried to forget the warnings she'd read about skiing off trails on this mountain—how treacherous crevasses could lie off the ski runs, ready to swallow up skiers. The wind bit at her cheeks, and she ducked her head slightly, trying to focus on the best pathway through the snow. At least the direction was easy—downhill.

They made better time now. The Vespers had longer

skis, faster on the trail but not as maneuverable as their shorter skis. Their path snaked through large boulders, and crags and cliffs lay on either side.

Amy squinted through her borrowed goggles. She saw a problem ahead. There were two natural divisions on the route they were on. To the right was a small stand of trees. To the left, large boulders rose through the snow, and the terrain grew increasingly rocky, ending in what appeared to be a huge crag that would qualify as an Olympic ski jump.

She went right. She heard Dan struggling for breath next to her as they tracked back and forth, finding a path through the trees. It should have brought them ahead, but it didn't. When they cleared the trees, she glanced behind. The two Vespers were right behind them. They would catch up in a few seconds.

She saw the inevitable end of this chase, and she pushed back against her panic.

Amy felt the ache in her legs and arms. Her muscles burned, and her chest hurt. She heard the sound she was dreading — Dan had started to wheeze. His breath was giving out.

Her muscles quivered. She gripped her poles and stared ahead fiercely, telling herself not to give up. When had she ever given up, even when she was exhausted and discouraged and sure she'd never succeed? That determination had kept her going. It had sustained them through the Clue hunt. Dan had it, too.

She glanced behind. The two skiers were moving so

fast. They were close enough now that she could hear the *schuss* of their skis. They weren't flailing like her and Dan. They were like machines.

Her leg muscles had gone past burning. They were shaking uncontrollably. The whole day had been too much, the lack of sleep, the shocks, the near-death experience. Amy felt tears well up and begin to fall.

They weren't going to make it.

She'd made the wrong choice, coming off the main trail. With another quick glance behind her, she could see that the Vespers were almost on them now.

Looming ahead, she saw an outcropping of snow, a small cliff, and she cried out to Dan and turned to miss it. They'd never make it over without falling. They made the turn, avoiding the outcropping, but the maneuver had cost them. The Vespers caught up.

It was over.

The Vespers stopped in front of them, turning in a spray of snow. Amy and Dan were forced to pull up. The only sound was their labored breathing and the hiss of the wind. She noticed how dusky it was, how the lights of the village seemed so far below them. How alone they were. To the left was the crag she'd avoided earlier. To the right, more forest. The snow ahead was wide and empty, but the Vespers blocked them from it.

Casper spoke. "The ring. That's all we want."

Was he telling the truth? They were certainly willing to send them plummeting to their deaths just a little while ago.

Amy gripped her ski poles while her mind worked frantically. Had she reached a dead end? If she handed over the ring, would there be a chance for them? She couldn't let anything happen to Dan. She was his older sister, his protector. He hated that, but it was true.

"Don't even think about it," Dan murmured to her. As usual, he knew what she was thinking—she would sacrifice the ring for him.

She felt the ring, snug on her thumb under her glove. Suddenly, in the midst of all this terror, she felt the shimmer of memories. One after the other, cascading down—Grace, her gaze so intent, handing her a new book in her library. Grace, lying on the window seat near the end, pain etched in every line on her face but turning to Amy and summoning up some inner light that somehow transformed her back into a vital person. Shielding Amy from her pain, shielding both of them from the terrible knowledge that death was in her bones and it was coming soon.

That was courage. That was strength.

How could she answer that with anything less?

"It's stuck," she told him. "I can't get it off my finger."

Casper withdrew a long, glittering knife. "Darling, that isn't a problem."

Suddenly, a dark shape appeared out of nowhere, flying so fast over the outcropping to their right that at first Amy thought it was a bird of prey instead of a skier.

Just as he hit the ground in a spray of snow, she felt movement to the other side. A snowboarder exploded off the rocky cliff to the left, twisting high in the air. He seemed to hang there for a long, extended moment. Casper nearly fell backward as he grabbed for his ski poles.

The snowboarder landed just inches away from Bruno, barreling into him and sending him airborne. Bruno landed on his back and began to slide.

"Whoa," Dan breathed.

Wyoming dug in his poles and took off. The skier changed direction and flew after him. Amy saw gray hair sticking out from the close-fitting wool hat. The amazing skier was Fiske!

Meanwhile, ahead of Wyoming, Bruno kept sliding. He must have hit an icy patch of snow. The mystery snowboarder was bearing down on him when suddenly Bruno disappeared. He was there one moment . . . and then gone. The snowboarder immediately turned his board and stopped.

It was too late for Wyoming. He was flying so fast on the ice that he went airborne for a moment and then he, too, disappeared. Fiske pulled up, the snow pluming out from the edges of his skis. He stood a minute, looking down.

Amy blinked. What had happened?

Cautiously, Amy and Dan skied closer. Fiske held up a hand so they stopped a few inches away from him and the snowboarder.

The snowboarder turned and said just one word. "Crevasse."

It was Erasmus.

●●●

They followed Erasmus and Fiske down the mountain, skiing slowly as the light faded. Amy's muscles were so tired that she had to use all her concentration to get down the mountain without falling.

They skied directly to the back porch of the chalet. Amy's fingers shook as she tried to get out of her ski boots. Fiske bent and gently helped her, then Dan, as Erasmus looked out over the twilight.

"Dude," Dan said tiredly to Erasmus. "A seven-twenty McTwist, and you nailed it. Awesome."

One corner of Erasmus's mouth lifted in a small smile. "Thanks. Dude."

Amy looked down at her uncle's gray head. He took off the second boot and rested his hand on her stocking foot. When he looked up, she smiled her thanks. He smiled back, but the smile was full of worry. He knew how close they'd come to disaster, just as she did.

But behind the worry, she saw something deep and rock steady. Love.

She stood up at the same time as Fiske, and he gathered her into a hug. She felt the surprising strength of his arms around her. He put one hand on her head and held her against his chest.

Fiske looked over Amy's head and extended an arm

at Dan. To Amy's surprise, her little brother didn't shrug or make a joke. He walked right into the hug. They stood in a small knot for a moment.

Amy closed her eyes and breathed in the scent of night air, pines, and snow. She'd been waiting for this moment since they'd got back from the Clue hunt. Through Thanksgiving and Christmas and early mornings and late nights, but somehow, the feelings had just missed the mark.

Now, the moment was here, and it rang through her heart, crystalline and perfect. *This is family.*

"Let's go inside and warm up," Fiske said.

Amy turned to thank Erasmus, but he was gone.

"He'll be watching the house tonight," Fiske said. "Just in case. We're taking the next train out, but we have time to rest before we go."

A fire blazed in the hearth, and there was a thermos of hot chocolate and a plate of sandwiches waiting.

"How is Frau Weiser?" Amy asked.

"She's already been released from the clinic," he said. "A head wound and a slight concussion. She'll be fine. Her daughter came up and did this for us."

They drank mugs of hot chocolate and gobbled up the sandwiches. Night had fallen fast, and the snow whispered against the panes.

"I've been thinking," Fiske said. "We've got to get rid of the ring. Maybe a London bank—"

"I've been thinking, too," Amy interrupted. "No more banks. That's what they'll expect us to do."

Fiske had already started shaking his head. "I know what you're thinking. You can't wear it, Amy. You'll be a target."

"I'm already a target," she argued. "Let's face it. And Grace chose me to protect it. 'Keep it close,' she said. Maybe the best way to do that is to hide it in plain sight."

Dan and Fiske gave her a questioning look. "How?" Dan asked.

Amy looked out the window at the black sky, the hard points of the stars, the dusting of golden lights on the lower slopes of the mountain. "Well," she said, "this *is* Switzerland, after all. . . ."

●●●●●

The snow had started last night and had been falling all day. Finally, it had snowed on a school day. Even the hardy city of Boston had come to a halt. Schools and businesses were closed. The wind had howled all night, pushing the snow into deep drifts.

Amy looked out her bedroom window. Grace's beautiful meadow was an expanse of white. Every tree and shrub was heavy with snow, the branches bent, scraping the ground as though they were bowing to applause for looking so beautiful.

Dusk was falling fast, the way it did in Massachusetts. She could smell something cooking downstairs. Fiske had promised a feast since they were snowed in.

She looked down at the watch on her wrist. Almost time for dinner. Her fingers trailed over the expensive Swiss timepiece. Each second ticked in a tiny, precise movement. Before heading home, they'd gone to the best watchmaker in Geneva.

The ring was now part of her, a gold circle for the black-faced watch.

She had protected the ring, and she would keep it safe.

They'd defeated the Vespers. Erasmus had passed a message to Fiske that they'd gone underground again . . . for now.

There was evidence that Casper Wyoming had escaped the fate of his companion. He was still out there.

She'd learned so much on the trip. The most important thing was this: She and Dan didn't know enough. They had almost died twice on that mountain, once because they'd made the wrong decision and once because they had overestimated their strength.

There had been too much luck involved in their success and too little skill.

They needed to be faster, smarter, better. They needed to know more. They needed to be good at more things. They needed to train. She remembered her burning muscles and lungs on that mountain, the feeling that her body couldn't do what she needed it to do.

That could never happen again.

Tonight, after dinner, she would tell Fiske, Nellie, and Dan what she'd been thinking about Grace's mansion.

She remembered how Dan had scoffed at Grace's note in the Swiss bank. He was right: Grace had never been sentimental. Renovating the house so that it looked exactly like it had when she was alive— it didn't make sense. Grace wouldn't approve of that. She'd snort at their foolishness.

They had to throw out all those plans Fiske had worked so hard on. They'd have to re-make Grace's mansion as theirs. A home, yes. But also a place to learn. A place to train. A place to get ready.

Amy felt the contours of the watch face, the ring that encircled the passage of time. She remembered Dan's face in the cable car, the thoughts crowding his head that only she could read. The serum. He had thought about it. It was racing around in her brother's head, and he must never, ever, be tempted by it again. He had to become strong *without* the serum. They both did.

They would need strength and skills and technology and training. Whatever they didn't know could be used against them. She would make it a game for Dan. She wouldn't tell him all her fears. She would give him as many more years of his childhood as she could.

But the reckoning would come. The Vespers were out there. And the next time they met, Amy vowed, she and Dan would be ready.